Marsh cleare

There was the
image of Ella standing beside her bed in the
lamplight, wearing only a skimpy bra and panties,
her hair tousled as if she'd been having wild sex—
how was he supposed to be immune to that? "It's
been a stressful time."

"I would agree with you."

"Under normal circumstances, I'd look at you and
see my best friend. But after all this drama, after
imagining you married to that scumbag and
potentially ending up pregnant with his child, I'm
more aware of you as a... woman."

"You didn't see me that way before?" She sounded
insulted.

"Of course, but in a general way."

"General? I'm not sure I like that, either. I'm not
some vague representation of a female human
being."

"I don't mean it like that." He was in the weeds. No
way out around it. "I didn't picture you having
sex."

TESTING THE COWBOY'S RESOLVE

ROWDY RANCH

Vicki Lewis Thompson

Ocean Dance Press

TESTING THE COWBOY'S RESOLVE
© 2022 Vicki Lewis Thompson

ISBN: 978-1-63803-947-1

Ocean Dance Press LLC
PO Box 69901
Oro Valley, AZ 85737

Visit the author's website at
VickiLewisThompson.com

_1_

Swearing under his breath, Marsh McLintock paced in front of Wagon Train's historic church, its coat of fresh white paint gleaming in the afternoon sun, the steeple lifting toward a cloudless blue Montana sky. Perfect weather for Ella Bradley's big day.

And the groom was late.

Marsh was ready to throttle him. Warner's flight had landed in Missoula two hours ago. According to Marsh's phone app, traffic on the 93 was moving just fine. Zero accidents. If Warner had missed the plane or had a snafu getting a rental car, wouldn't he have texted Ella?

But she'd heard nothing, so she'd asked him to come outside and watch for the guy. Marsh was only too glad to do it. He'd use his twenty seconds of privacy with the inconsiderate jerk to blast him for leaving a whole bunch of folks, including his bride, twiddling their thumbs.

His heart ached for her. She'd been so excited about this wedding. The short engagement had fit her schedule perfectly since she'd be back to teaching in September.

Planning the event on short notice hadn't been easy, but she'd relished every minute. He should know. He'd helped her with most of it. Warner had claimed he was too busy building up his insurance agency.

With her folks on a long-awaited dream trip through Europe and her sister Faye committed to a Shakespeare summer festival in Seattle, Marsh had been the logical backup. He and Ella had been buddies since kindergarten.

He'd been secretly relieved when Warner had waltzed down to Florida for a month of sales training. Working with Ella was easier when her fiancé wasn't around.

They'd had everything running like clockwork until Warner announced he couldn't leave Florida until this morning. Nobody would be available to pick him up at the airport, so he'd have to hire a rental, but he'd said that was fine. Supposedly he needed the time in Miami to finalize a big insurance deal.

Ella had defended his choice, so Marsh had kept his mouth shut But this... being late and not bothering to communicate... there was no excuse.

"Marsh." Faye hurried out of a side door in her teal maid-of-honor dress. She'd inherited her mom's brunette hair while Ella was a blonde like her dad.

"Did he text?"

"Not yet, and—"

"Damn it, Faye. He'd better be unconscious in a ditch somewhere. Otherwise, he's the most inconsiderate—"

"Inconsiderate doesn't even begin to cover it." She handed over her phone. "Take a look at this."

He glanced at the image. Then he studied it more closely. A dark-haired woman in a bikini was plastered against a blond guy in swim trunks kissing him for all she was worth. While taking a selfie. "Please tell me that's not—"

"Sure is. There are more where you can ID him, but this is the most blatant clinch. She posted them on her page an hour ago."

His stomach cramped. "Who is she?"

"Her name's Dinah. Lives in Miami and works for the same insurance company as Warner. I've been following her online ever since he made some reference to her on his page about three weeks ago. He wouldn't dare post something like this, but she did. Fortunately she didn't tag him, so only her contacts will see it."

"You haven't shown Ella?"

"I wanted you to be with me when I do."

"Maybe they were just fooling around. Maybe—"

"And maybe she's the reason he delayed coming back until today."

"We don't know that."

She met his gaze. "I think we do. Tell me the truth. Didn't you peg him as a weasel from the get-go?"

"Yes, ma'am, but I hoped I was—"

"Me, too, but we weren't wrong."

"There's still a chance this could be explained."

"But he won't have to if we don't show her the picture. We need to do it now or never."

"Then now it is." He sucked in a breath and handed back her phone. "If it's a misunderstanding, he can explain when he gets here."

"Wanna bet it's not a misunderstanding?"

"I want it to be." He followed her to the side door of the church. "She loves him. She believes in him. She—"

"She's gullible. We both know that. And he's a smooth talker. Great salesman. That's why he's attracted the attention of the big brass. Ella would make the perfect corporate wife, so he—"

"She won't thank us, Faye."

"I know. I can take it."

His body tightened, as if bracing for a blow. "Me, too. But I hate this for her." He caught her arm before they reached the door. "Wait. Who's in there with her?"

"Just Mom and Brit, unless someone else popped in after I left."

"Did you tell either of them you were watching this woman's posts?"

"I didn't tell anyone. What if I was wrong? But when I saw this one I came straight out here to get you. She'll take the news better if you're there."

"We should probably ask her to step out of the room instead of showing it to her in front of your mom and Brit."

"Okay."

"Let me see the picture again. If we stir things up and it turns out to be a joke or no big deal, I'll feel like a—"

"Let me show you the rest. The relationship is pretty clear." She tapped on her phone. "Oh, hell, she's put up another one — the two of them cuddling on a beach towel. And she tagged him." She scrolled backward. "She edited the other ones and tagged him there, too. Maybe she forgot before."

He looked over her shoulder and his gut clenched. "In other words, she wants his contacts to see these."

"Specifically, Ella."

"We'd better get in there." He reached for the door.

"Looks like revenge. Like he led her along and at the last minute announced he was getting married."

"That would be cold." He followed Faye inside.

"But it would explain—" She was cut off by Ella's cry of dismay. "She just saw it."

Damn.

The hall door flew open and Ella charged out, holding up the skirt of her wedding dress, her blue eyes wide with shock. "Marsh! Oh, my God, is he here yet? This can't be happening! He wouldn't— I can't believe—"

"Maybe it's a bad joke." Marsh closed the distance between them and took her by the shoulders. The white lace under his palms disoriented him. She never wore lacey stuff.

"More like a mean joke." She was breathing hard. "She altered those pictures. I'm sure she did."

"Easy enough these days." Her mom, nearly as tall as her daughters, hurried out of the room, fire in her eyes. "What an awful thing to do."

Brit stepped out from behind Ella's mom. She barely came up to Liz Bradley's shoulder, even with her dark hair in a bridesmaid's updo. "I'm guessing she came on to him and he turned her down, so this is how she—"

"Oh, here he is." Liz gestured toward the open side door. "Thank goodness you've arrived, Warner. I'm afraid you're the victim of a social media attack."

Marsh let go of Ella and turned as Warner stepped inside.

"Social media's so jacked up. You can't believe anything you see on there." Ella's fiancé didn't look so good. He'd been attacked, all right, but social media wouldn't have left a big puffy bruise on his cheek. "Hey, everybody!" His attempt to pull off a hearty smile didn't go well. His wince of pain was obvious. "Sorry I'm late."

Marsh figured he'd stopped along the way to buy makeup, but it couldn't disguise the damage. His bloodshot eyes looked like the result of a long, boozy night, followed by a hard slap by an enraged woman.

"Warner, honey, you're hurt." Ella went to him. "What happened, sweetheart? Was there a brawl on the plane?"

"Um, yeah, exactly. Don't know what this world is coming to. Just give me a minute to change into my duds and we'll do this thing. Your dress is lovely, Ella."

Marsh exchanged a glance with Faye. She looked ready to strangle Warner with her bare hands. He mouthed *I've got this.* He'd offer to help Warner change. And get the truth out of the bastard by whatever means necessary. There would be no wedding today if he had anything to say about it.

"I hope the ceremony won't be too much stress after what you've been through." Ella gently stroked his cheek, the undamaged one.

"It's nothing compared to the stress of postponing it, my love. You're my heart, my soul."

Marsh wanted to barf.

"Okay, then." Ella smiled. "It's not like we could easily take a raincheck. Thank you for soldiering on..." She paused and her fingers trailed to his open collar. Drawing it aside, she gasped. Then she slowly lifted her gaze to his. "You have a hickey." She said it calmly, almost conversationally.

"I do? That can't be right. You know, when I was taking a shower this morning, the shampoo bottle fell and caught me on the neck. I'll bet that's what—"

"Shut up, Warner." Her voice quivered with fury. "I'm not stupid. You didn't get hit by a shampoo bottle."

"Okay, so a cocktail waitress got a little too friendly."

"Is her name Dinah, by chance?"

"Who's Dinah?"

Faye shoved her phone in front of his face. "Allow me to introduce you."

His eyes widened. "Um..."

"That showed up on my phone, too." Ella's blue eyes glittered. "I thought it was a prank."

"Which it is, my love. Just a stupid prank. That's all it—"

"And the hickey? Is that part of the prank, too?"

"Like I said—"

"There was no brawl on the plane, was there?"

"Not exactly."

"Just how dumb do you think I am?"

His expression turned sheepish. "Oh, c'mon, Ella. You know how guys are. One last fling before we tie the knot. Means *nothing*. It's traditional to—"

"Did your friend Dinah know she was part of this grand old male tradition? Judging from that ginormous bruise, I think not."

"Oh, she knew, all right." He switched from jovial to accusatory. "Hell, I was only there for a month. If she made assumptions, that's on her. I had temporary written all over me."

"And guess what's written all over you now, Warner? Here's a hint. It's a body part that starts with A and ends with E."

"You're upset, sweetheart. I can see that. Let's just get through the ceremony and then we'll have a heart-to-heart. We'll work it out. Every couple has their ups and—"

"Are you freaking kidding me? I would rather marry our famous wooden buffalo than you, Warner Stapleton the Third!"

"Ella, please. We can—"

"The wedding won't be happening, but the reception will, and you're not invited!"

"Aw, Ella, baby. Don't be this way."

"Suck it, Warner." She turned to her mom and paused to clear her throat. "I'm willing to announce the change in plans to our guests, but it might be less dramatic if you and Dad handled that. Meanwhile the four of us will head over to the Buffalo."

"We can do that, honey." Liz gave her a quick hug. "You kids go on and get situated. We'll be along."

"My truck's right out front." Marsh pulled his keys from his pocket. Since he'd been scheduled to drive the happy couple to the reception, he'd detailed it and parked it close.

"Just let me grab our purses." Brit dashed back into the room.

Warner looked befuddled. "What am I supposed to do?"

Marsh had a suggestion. Instead he took the high road. "You might want to notify your parents, your brother, and your best friend, who all spent their time and money to fly out here."

"Right." He hesitated. "Can they come to the reception?"

"Ask Ella. She's in charge."

Ella glanced at Warner as if he were a nasty mess on the floor. "I wouldn't mind, except I can't imagine they'd have much fun. We'll be trash-talking about you all night."

"You'd better text your relatives instead of going into the chapel, Warner." Liz sent him a glare hot enough to melt steel. "I doubt you want to be around when Ella's dad finds out about this. Gerald's normally a mild-mannered guy. But when someone hurts a member of his family, he—"

"Good point." He ducked out the door, leaving it open.

Faye rushed over to peer out. "Guess he's not a total dummy. He's running."

"Oh, he's a total dummy," Marsh said. "He cheated on Ella. You can't get any dumber than that."

"Thanks." She gave him a tiny smile. "Ready to party?"

"You know it, Ellabella."

"Then let's go make some noise."

That was his Ella, putting on a good show even if her heart was shattered. He'd help her get plastered tonight, and he'd stick around to pick up the pieces tomorrow. That's what friends were for.

2

Adrenaline left Ella shaky and clumsy. Her voluminous skirt nearly tripped her up as she attempted the climb into Marsh's truck. But his firm grip on her arm guided her safely into the passenger seat.

Normally she got herself in and out of his truck, but not today. She glanced down. "Thanks. I'm a little wobbly."

His kind eyes were filled with understanding. "You're allowed." He gave her arm a squeeze. "You reduced him to ashes. Well done."

"Epic kiss-off speech," Brit climbed into the backseat of the four-door truck.

"Just wish Marsh had decked him, though." Faye got in the other side.

"I would've loved to." He helped Ella tuck her skirt inside the truck. "But then we'd be stuck with his sorry ass. I wanted him gone, not unconscious on the floor."

Faye sighed. "You're right. That would have been awkward."

"And besides," Ella said, "he's not worth getting your shirt dirty."

He gave her a grim smile. "Definitely not."

It was one of their private jokes. As kids they'd devoured reruns of *Maverick*, starring the suave gambler who was famous for defeating the bad guy without mussing his clothes.

Closing the door, Marsh rounded the hood and swung into the driver's seat. "Fluffy Buffalo, here we come."

He sounded cheerful, but his tight jaw and rigid body told a different story. Punching Warner to avenge her honor would have released that tension.

But he was a McLintock. All nine of those brothers had impressive muscles, but using them to settle a dispute was always a last resort.

As Marsh backed the truck out of the parking space, she wrangled her skirt so it wouldn't spill over the console and interfere with his driving. "We should call the Buffalo and let them know the situation."

"I'll do it," Faye said.

"You can if you want." Marsh pulled onto the road. "But I'll bet Clint's been in touch with Tyra ever since it was obvious the wedding would be delayed." He met Faye's gaze in the rearview mirror. "Once your folks make their announcement, he'll likely got on the phone."

"You're right. I had mentally filed him under *wedding guest* and sort of forgot he's the manager there. But even if he's alerted Tyra, he won't know Ella's preferences."

"He doesn't need to." She swiveled in her seat so she could look at her sister. "Marsh and I arranged everything weeks ago."

"Yeah, but you might want to change a few things, like the congratulations banner. Do you still want—"

"Yes." She ignored the sick feeling in her stomach. The adrenaline shakes were fading and reality was setting in. "It still works. Congratulations to me for dodging a bullet."

"For sure, girlfriend." Brit settled back with a sigh. "This is awful, but the alternative would have been way worse."

"I totally agree," Faye said. "Tonight we celebrate my big sis's narrow escape from the clutches of a slimy troll. But you might want to rethink the music selections you gave the band."

"Oh. Forgot about that." The playlist had to go. Her despicable fiancé had betrayed her, destroying their fairytale ending. How could he? And how could she have been so blind? Their moments of intimacy soured in her stomach like a fancy meal loaded with salmonella.

"These folks are talented musicians," Brit said. "I'm sure they can switch gears and give us a lot of fun stuff and plenty of sassy line dances. Maybe we should tell them to play the same tunes they did for Ella's bachelorette party."

Faye nodded. "Excellent suggestion." She glanced at Ella. "You good with that idea?"

She managed a smile. "Works for me." Her bachelorette party a week ago had been a blast. She'd been on top of the world, eager to start her new life with a man who adored her. Except he hadn't adored her enough to be faithful.

Faye gave her a long look. Then she shook her head. "You know what? We don't need to hear what they played for the bachelorette party. We'll see if they can give us the same vibe, just different numbers."

"The bachelorette tunes are fine." Ella pulled herself back from the abyss. "I doubt they have an unlimited repertoire." She faced forward again to avoid looking at Faye. Sympathy was liable to jumpstart the waterworks.

"You never know until you ask." Faye had her fake happy voice going on. "I'll make the request and say it's fine if they need to repeat a few of those bachelorette songs."

"But they should put them toward the end of the evening," Brit said. "By then we'll have consumed enough booze to neutralize the nostalgia. Right, Ella?"

"Right." She'd agree to whatever they'd been saying. She'd lost focus. Or not lost it, exactly, but switched to a different channel, the one that played the image of Warner getting cozy on a beach towel with someone named Dinah.

She should probably feel sorry for that woman, who'd been duped just like she had. Even better, she should send the lady an online message and thank her for shining a light on Warner's deceit.

Maybe tomorrow. She didn't have the bandwidth now. Rage and grief for her own self occupied every square inch of her being. All her beautiful plans were— Warner's ringtone filled the cab. "Dammit!" She twisted toward the backseat. "Brit, where's my purse?"

"Here." She handed it up to the front.

Wrenching it open, Ella yanked out her phone. "He's so blocked!" She tapped the screen quickly and sank back against the seat, gasping with outrage. "I can't effing believe he did that."

Faye reached up and squeezed her shoulder. "If you'll give me your phone, I'll delete his contact info."

Taking a shaky breath, she let it out slowly. "That would be great." She handed it into the backseat. "Thanks." Then she turned and held out her purse to Brit. "If you'd hang onto this for me, that would be a huge help. I have all I can manage with this pup tent of a skirt."

"Be glad to take charge of it."

"Oh, and while I'm at it...." She tugged off her engagement ring and rolled down her window, prepared to fling it as far as it would go.

"Don't." Faye's command stopped her. "Sell it online. Donate the money to the Wagon Train basketball program."

"Great idea, but in the meantime—"

"Give it to me," Marsh said. "I'll put it in my pocket."

"Okay." She handed over the ring and rolled up her window.

Gradually her heart rate slowed, but her ears were plugged as if she was on a mountain road. When Marsh spoke her name, she could barely hear him. She glanced over, then shifted her gaze to the back seat.

Faye was engrossed in a conversation with someone at the Buffalo and Brit was eavesdropping on the call and making additional suggestions. She returned her attention to Marsh. "What?"

"You don't have to go through with it." He kept his voice low. "Faye and Brit will make your excuses and I can take you home. Going ahead with the party is brilliant, but you don't have to be there."

"I don't want to be alone, either."

"You won't be. I'll stay with you. We can get stinkin' drunk."

"That sounds great."

"Then let's—"

"But I have my pride. Like Coach Blake always said — *never let 'em see you sweat.*"

"She was talking about basketball. This isn't—"

"I know, but… it feels like hiding in the locker room while the game's on the line."

"Folks would understand. But it's your call." He idled beside a reserved spot in front of the Buffalo. An employee came out and removed the orange cones blocking it so he could pull in.

"Nice job on the parking spot." She and Marsh had arranged this with Tyra, the Buffalo's owner, last week. As per their instructions, the staff had roped off the area with teal and white ribbons to match the wedding's color scheme. Teal pots of white roses lined the curb.

"Sorry you didn't spring for a limo?"

"No way. An equine vet's work truck is way more interesting."

He shut off the motor and glanced at her. "Well?"

Sitting in what looked like the winner's circle at the Kentucky Derby, she was so tempted to take his suggestion and bail. But Coach Blake had come to the wedding and would doubtless be at the reception. She lifted her chin. "I'm staying."

Admiration flashed in his dark eyes. "Way to go, champ."

She'd always cherished that look. She'd been treated to it after every game in high school, win or lose. Next to her family, he'd been her biggest fan.

"The band's fine with giving us new tunes," Faye said. "They've written several songs they rarely get to perform because people want the popular ones."

"That's exactly what we need," Ella said. "New songs, original music. I can't wait to hear it."

"Sounds like we're ready." Marsh opened his door and glanced into the back seat. "If you'll both stay put, I'll be around to help you out."

"Thanks, but I'm fine, Marsh." Faye opened her door.

"Same here," Brit said. "Just get Ella. That skirt is epic."

She sighed. "You've got that right. I feel like Scarlett O'Hara. I didn't factor in the ride to the Buffalo. Or dancing! How am I supposed to dance in this?"

"We'll figure something out." Marsh grabbed his hat from the dash, climbed down and closed the door.

She watched with envy as Faye and Brit hurried toward the Buffalo in dresses that swirled around their knees.

Opening her door, Marsh held out his hand. "Just take it slow."

She placed her hand in his reassuring grip. "Next time I decide to get married, I'm wearing shorts and a T-shirt."

"Just so you know, you look amazing in that dress."

"Thanks. I just wish I could see where I'm putting my feet."

"You know what? I'll lift you out." He let go of her hand. "That way I can make sure you won't take a tumble."

"Okay."

"Duck your head and put your hands on my shoulders."

She tipped her head down and held onto him. He felt good, solid, trustworthy. What would she have done today without Marsh?

He grasped her around the waist. "Good Lord, what've you got on under this dress?"

"A corset. It's supposed to make the dress fit more smoothly."

"Can you breathe?"

"Sort of."

"Okay, then. Here goes." He swung her down to the pavement. "Got your feet under you?"

"Yes." She lifted her head. He had such nice eyes, a warm, expressive brown. And long dark lashes she'd always envied.

He loosened his grip on her waist but didn't let go. She didn't want him to, at least not yet. His touch steadied her. And reminded her how much she hated the corset.

He smiled. "You're gonna be fine, Ellabella."

"Yeah." Why not kiss him? He'd been so sweet about this disaster. Rising on her toes, she pressed her mouth against his. His lips had a velvety texture. Supple. Becoming warmer. She lingered.

His sudden intake of breath startled her. She pulled back. "Sorry. Probably shouldn't have done that."

An emotion flickered in his eyes. "No worries. You've had a shock."

"That must be it. I didn't mean to make things weird."

"You didn't."

"I hope not." She heaved a sigh. "Because my world just got rearranged and if I somehow screwed up my relationship with you just now, that would be the last straw."

"You can't screw up our relationship. It's bulletproof."

That made her grin. "Covered in Kevlar?"

"Absolutely." He let go of her.

She let go of him, too. As she moved back, she stepped on the hem of her dress. She threw out her arms and regained her balance. "This skirt is a hazard."

"Let's get you inside. Then we'll work on solutions to the dress problem." He offered his arm. "Grab on. We just need to make it through the door."

"Assuming I'll fit." She looped her arm through his and they started toward the entrance. "I promise not to kiss you again."

He laughed. "Was it that bad?"

"I didn't say that. It's just... kissing is not our thing."

"No, it hasn't been."

Hmm. Was she imagining the slight huskiness in his voice?

A ripple of awareness caught her by surprise. Wait. This was Marsh. Squiggly sensations in her stomach weren't part of their dynamic any more than kissing was.

Okay, he was right. She'd had a shock. Once it wore off, they'd be back to normal.

3

Ella was vulnerable. Not herself. Marsh told himself that several times as they made their way to the entrance, where a sign that read *Private Party in Progress* hung on the door.

With some jockeying, he managed to fit her and her big skirt through the opening without catching the delicate material on a splinter or a loose nail. The age of the building meant either one might be present and could put a large rip in her beautiful dress.

She looked like an angel in that thing. He'd been tamping down his reaction to Ella in her wedding dress ever since he'd gone with her for the final fitting. The sight of her coming out of the fitting room had nearly brought him to his knees.

In that moment he couldn't avoid the truth any longer. He was in love with Ella Bradley. A little late in the game to be admitting it to himself. She'd been days away from marrying another man.

But Warner was out of the picture. And Ella had just kissed him.

Unfortunately, it had been a knee-jerk reaction brought on by emotional trauma, not a major shift in the way she thought about him. She was hurting. He'd be an idiot to put faith in anything she said or did right now. He needed to forget about that kiss. Yeah, that wasn't gonna happen. His lips still tingled.

As they passed hidden sensors at the entrance, the large wooden buffalo bellowed *Welcooome tooo the paaartayyy.* Clearly the buffalo had been reprogrammed for this event.

Ella glanced at him. "Did you request that new message?"

"Nope. I was thinking you did."

"Not me. Probably Clint or Tyra." She surveyed the area. "Seems strange to see the place empty at this hour on a Saturday. I mean, empty except for Brit, Faye and Cecily. They look busy over there."

"Probably rearranging the place cards."

"Yes, we are," Faye called out. "We wanted to set Warner's on fire, but Cecily wouldn't let us."

"That's for sure." Cecily, the blonde who'd waited tables at the Buffalo for years, left her task and came over to greet them. "No open flame allowed in this creaky old building."

Ella nodded. "l remember. No candles on the birthday cakes."

"No, ma'am. Anyway, I'm sorry about... everything." She gave Ella a sympathetic smile. "Men suck." Then she blushed and turned to Marsh. "Except for *you*, of course! You're wonderful. And your brothers are wonderful, too. I didn't mean to say that *all*—"

"It's okay, Cecily. One bad apple can make us all look rotten."

"Not true. It makes some look even better. Right, Ella?"

"Matter of fact, it does." She didn't look at him and her cheeks turned pinker than Cecily's.

Was she embarrassed that she'd kissed him? Quite likely. He'd let her know it would be their little secret.

"I thought I heard you guys come in." Tyra hurried out of her office. The air always seemed to crackle around her. Six years ahead of them in school, she'd been class president, head cheerleader and valedictorian. "The band just pulled up out back. They texted me that the music situation is handled."

Ella nodded. "Faye and Brit talked to them."

"And by the way, that dress is stunning on you."

"I've tried to tell her that." Marsh said. "But she—"

"I appreciate the compliments, guys. You're very kind, but I'm so over dragging this skirt around. Tyra, is there any chance you have some sturdy scissors in your office?"

Cecily's eyes widened. "You are *not* going to cut that skirt down. That would be a—"

"Hold it, sis." Faye headed their way. "Just hold your horses, little lady. You're not taking scissors to that dress. Not on my watch."

"It's not like I'll ever wear it again." She paused. "Do you want it?"

"Not me. I've seen how you struggle. But you could donate it to a clothing bank."

"I pity the woman who ends up with it. Pretty to look at, impossible to walk in, let alone dance."

"Maybe so." Cecily stood back and gave it a once-over. "But I guarantee some woman will be thrilled to have it. I see your point, though. It takes up a lot of space."

"Exactly. Can you imagine the pileup if I get out on the floor?"

"I can." Tyra grinned. "Would be fun to watch."

"Then I hope the Buffalo's insurance is paid up."

"You didn't bring something to change into for the reception?"

"I did not. That's one detail that escaped me." She turned to him. "I thought we had everything covered."

"You know what? Your house is minutes away. What if I make a quick trip to your place and grab something from your closet?"

She looked at him and blinked. "Brilliant. Thank you. My blue sleeveless dress would be perfect."

"You can use my office to change," Tyra said. "I might even have something I can put the dress in temporarily, so it'll be easier to transport."

"Wonderful." She turned back to Marsh. "You just saved the day again. Or rather, the night."

"What about shoes?"

She lifted her skirt. "These will work. I was smart about that, at least."

"Okay, then. I'll be back before you know it." He dug out his keys and started toward the door.

"Oh, one more thing."

He swung around. "A jacket for the trip home?"

"No." She hurried toward him, holding her skirt up to keep from tripping. "The nights are still warm enough." She drew closer and lowered her voice. "But I'd love to ditch this corset. My boring bras are in the top drawer of my dresser, left-hand side. I'll be eternally grateful if you'd bring me one."

"One boring bra, coming up." She was regaining their normal buddy-buddy status. She'd asked about the bra without blushing.

"Be sure and grab one from the left-hand pile, not a lacy one from the other side. I am not feeling sexy tonight."

Message received, Ella. That kiss was an outlier she wanted to forget about. "Got it."

"Thanks, Marsh." She met his gaze. "We'll laugh about this someday."

Another one of their favorite catch phrases. Yep, she was giving off nothing but buddy vibes, now. "Hell, I'm laughing about it, now. I'll be back in a flash — your dress on a hanger and your bra stuffed in my pocket."

She grinned. "I owe you one."

"I'll keep that in mind." Touching two fingers to the brim of his Stetson, he headed out the door.

Whatever had prompted that kiss, she clearly didn't want to follow up on it. And rightly so. The last thing she needed right now was a new lover. She needed a friend, though. He had that role down cold. He'd stick to it.

As he backed his truck out of the reserved spot, Gerald and Liz's SUV appeared around the corner and headed his way. The same employee who'd removed the cones replaced them once he'd cleared the space. Looks like he'd have it when he returned. That would save time.

If the evening went as expected, he'd be escorting a tipsy Ella out to his truck. Having it smack-dab in front of the entrance would be convenient.

Good thing he still had his key for this errand. He'd offered to give it back when she and Warner got engaged, but she'd asked him to hang onto it until after the wedding since he was so involved in the preparations. And sure enough, his key was coming in han— what the hell?

The car Warner had been running toward sat in the driveway. And Warner wasn't in it.

Bile rose in his throat. Ella's ex also had a key. Swerving to the curb, he cut the engine and exited the truck, ready for battle.

He was on the front porch in seconds, his breath coming fast. Then he paused. Barreling in there without a plan wasn't the smartest move.

Warner's presence here was proof of his self-delusion, which could lead to all kinds of unpredictable behavior. Was he cagey enough to lock the door after him? Nope. The knob turned easily.

Body coiled, Marsh cracked the door open a couple inches. The rasp of Warner's loud snore lowered his tension but raised his level of disgust. What a gold-plated bastard.

He slipped inside and left the door standing open. Warner was down for the count. He hadn't even bothered to take off the jacket he'd had on when he'd arrived at the church. Must have come straight here and made himself at home. The dead soldiers on the coffee table testified that he'd chugged three of Ella's beers before passing out. What a gem.

With his booted feet propped on the table, his body slumped against the cushions, his head lolling back and his open mouth emitting a gag-worthy stench, he'd make any marriage-minded woman revise her plans. His cheating was only one of many reasons not to hook up with this loser.

Marsh took off his Stetson and hung it on the coat rack by the door. Ella would have to wait a little longer for her dress and bra.

Careful to make no sound, he crossed to the coffee table and pocketed the key lying there. He moved the empty bottles and the small pot of African violets to the fireplace hearth. Then he kicked Warner's feet off the table.

The guy pitched forward with a startled cry and clutched his head. "What the—"

"On your feet, Stapleton."

He lifted his head, his gaze unfocused. "McLintock?"

Marsh's blood turned to ice. "On. Your. Feet."

"This isn't your house."

"It's not yours, either, asshole. Get out."

"She gave me a key." He glanced at the coffee table. "Hey, did you—"

"You can leave on your own or I can throw you out." He flexed his fingers. "Your choice."

"Whatcha doing here, anyway?"

"None of your business. Out."

"You can't order me around." He settled back on the couch. "I'm Ella's fiancé. She and I need to talk. Since she blocked my calls, I decided to—"

"Time's up." Grabbing the front of his jacket, Marsh yanked him to his feet and spun him around. Wow, the guy smelled like a garbage dump. He'd rather wrestle with a stubborn equine patient any day.

"Let go! You can't—"

"Watch me." He pressed his forearm against Warner's throat and pinned his arm behind his back at an angle guaranteed to deliver pain. Once he'd immobilized the creep, he shoved him toward the open door.

Warner struggled to get loose, but booze and exhaustion worked against him. Even without those handicaps, he would have been toast. Marsh's hours on the weight bench this summer were coming in handy.

"I'll bring charges!" Warner choked out the words, hampered by Marsh's arm across his larynx.

"I think not."

"I sure as hell will! This is assault!"

"You already stand to lose business because of how you treated Ella." Marsh propelled him down the steps and across the lawn to his car, hauling him upright whenever he stumbled.

"Prosecute me and you'll be finished in Wagon Train."

"I'll sue for defamation!"

"Here's what you'll do, Stapleton." Tightening his hold on the guy's neck, he released his arm and opened the driver's door. Then he stepped back. "You'll get in that car and drive home. And you'll stay away from Ella. Permanently."

Massaging his arm, Warner turned around in an unsteady show of bravado. "You can't make that stick."

Marsh locked his gaze with Warner's. "Don't test me."

Whatever circles of hell the guy saw in his eyes must have scared him. He scooted into the car, slammed the door and hit the locks.

Seconds later the engine roared and he backed out of the drive without checking for traffic. Lucky for him nobody was coming. A wreck would have complicated things.

Marsh shook out both hands as if that could rid him of the cooties he'd picked up from Warner. A shower and change of clothes would be nice. No chance. Dragging in a breath, he walked back inside, shivering as adrenaline coursed through his body.

How much time had he lost? Minutes stretched into hours during a confrontation. In reality, hauling Warner out of Ella's house likely took less than ten minutes. Ella would be busy talking to people. She wouldn't notice how long he'd been gone. Or ask questions.

He straightened his vest and picked up his Stetson. Good thing he hadn't dirtied his shirt.

4

Ella glanced out the streetside windows of the Buffalo. Her parents' SUV and Coach Baker's Jeep had just pulled in. She turned back to Faye and Brit. "The guests are coming. I'll go stand by the entrance and greet everyone as they arrive."

"Not by yourself, you won't." Faye walked over and linked her arm through Ella's. "Brit and I will be your lieutenants."

"Damn straight." Brit stationed herself on Ella's other side. "And we'll be a vast improvement over the idiot who was supposed to stand next to you in this receiving line."

Ella smiled. "That's for sure."

"We're ready," Tyra said. "Brandy's behind the bar and my other server is here. The band's tuned up. Should I give them the signal to start?"

Ella nodded. "By all means." The musicians launched into a country tune she hadn't heard before. Might be one of their own. Marsh would be back any minute. She could do this.

Her parents were the first two people through the door. They didn't pause for even a second. Arms outstretched, they gathered all three members of the reception line into a group hug.

Ella gulped back tears. If she started crying now, she might never stop.

"Hell of a thing." Her dad's voice was gruff with emotion as he stepped away and cleared his throat. "He might as well leave town. All our friends who switched to his agency are not only cancelling, they're passing the word to everybody they know."

"As well they should," her mom said. "Our family has a lifetime of ties to this community. Warner turned a plus into a minus."

"Poor guy." Brit exchanged an evil grin with Faye. "He spent so much money renovating that office space. What ever will he do when he can't make his business loan payments?"

"I hear they're hiring at Buns and Beer," Faye said. "Although they might not take him on. The manager's a friend of mine."

"The word's just beginning to spread." Brit glanced around the still-empty room. "By the time this gathering is over, he'll be lucky if he can get served at the Buns and Beer, let alone be hired to flip burgers."

"But we wouldn't have known without the posts from Dinah this afternoon," Faye said. "Without her intervention, Ella would be married to that cheating SOB and we'd be toasting their happiness tonight."

Ella shuddered. "You're right, sis. We should send her a thank-you from the whole family."

"Good thought. We'll talk about it later." Her dad tipped his head toward the group of wedding guests crowded at the entrance waiting for the chance to greet the almost-bride. "We need to move aside so all those folks can give you some love."

"Then open the floodgates." As her parents left to find their table, Ella surveyed the crowd. Her gaze locked with Serena Blake's. Her high school coach gave her two-thumbs up and smiled. Yep, staying for the reception had been the right call.

But focusing on the guests who wanted to offer their condolences was a little like rubbing salt in the wound. And where was Marsh? She kept an eye on the reserved parking space, looking for his white truck.

It wasn't as if she could change the minute he arrived. She'd have to wait until after she'd greeted everyone. But she felt calmer when he was nearby.

Gradually she adjusted to the flow of sympathy from friends and family. Some were better at striking the right note than others.

Beau McLintock came through the door with his trademark smile and his very pregnant wife, Jess. She did her best to hug Ella, Faye and Brit. They all ended up with the giggles.

"At least I didn't give birth this morning," Jess said. "I was hoping she'd show up last week, so I wouldn't have to wear maternity clothes today, but she had other ideas."

"Well, her name is Maverick, after all," Faye said.

"I hope I don't live to regret giving in to Beau on that."

"I love the name," Brit said. "It guarantees she won't be boring."

"Exactly!" Beau put his arm around Jess's shoulders. "That was my goal. Hey, where's Marsh? I asked if we could have that reserved spot since his truck's not there and we're extremely pregnant, but they said he'd be back and they had their instructions."

"Those are old instructions," Ella said. "Please go tell them I said you could park there. There's no need for Marsh to hang onto that spot."

"Thank you kindly, ma'am. I'll do that after I get the mother of our child settled with the non-alcoholic beverage of her choice. I hope Marsh didn't have a vet emergency."

"Not that I know of. He just ran over to my house to pick up a change of clothes so I won't be stuck in this dress all night."

Jess nodded. "I almost made that same mistake. Figured it out at the last minute."

"I figured it out like twenty minutes ago."

Beau nodded. "And my little brother charged to the rescue, riding his trusty white steed. Sounds just like him. Okay, we'll move out of the way and let other folks love on you." He gave Ella another hug. "Be happy. It's your best revenge against the bastard."

"Great advice." She turned to welcome one of her friends from UM. About five minutes later, Beau's red truck pulled into the parking space reserved for the bride and groom. She was glad he'd said something because in her current state she might not have thought to give them the parking space.

Soon after Beau parked, he came in with Marsh, who was carrying her blue dress on a hanger. He laughed at something Beau said. He also looked considerably more relaxed.

Time away from the wedding-related action might have been good for him. He tended to worry when she was stressed. If the errand had given him a much-needed break, so much the better.

As Beau waved at her and headed for the table where Jess sat with his family, Marsh came over and held up the dress. "I hope this is it. I didn't realize you had more than one blue dress."

"That's it." She took it from him. "Thank you so much for fetching it. I wanted the sleeveless one since it gets hot on the dance floor, especially during fast two-steps." She met his gaze. "You're the best. I really appreciate this."

"You're welcome. No trouble at all."

"I think you can go change," Faye said. "Just about everybody's here. Brit and I'll help you."

"We sure will. Let's free you from your dress so we can all start dancing to the great music they've been playing."

Ella glanced over at the empty dance floor. "Why isn't anybody dancing now?"

"My guess is they're waiting for you, toots," Faye said.

"Me? Surely they know there won't be a traditional bride and groom dance."

"Even if they know that, they might not feel right partying out there until you're ready to join them."

"That's nuts. I'll go make an announcement that they can—"

"Or." Brit glanced at Marsh. "You can add some flair to the occasion by leading off the dancing with your good buddy Marsh. Everyone would love that."

"Oh, they would." Faye smiled. "That's a fabulous idea. You guys are amazing on the floor. Let's think of a fun number."

"Oh, I've got one." Ella glanced at Marsh. "*Before He Cheats.* You up for this?"

"You know I am."

Faye clapped her hands together. "I love it! Marsh, you can make the request while we pry Ella out of her dress."

"Okay, but I have—"

"Come with us." Ella tipped her head in the direction of Tyra's office. "Just as far as Tyra's office."

"Huh?" Faye's eyebrows lifted. "Why does he have to—"

"Because..." Ella lowered her voice. "He has my comfy bra in his pocket."

"Oh." Faye snorted. "Well, that's what friends are for, isn't it? Way to go, Marsh."

"Thanks."

"He's a lifesaver." Ella led the way, walking as fast as her yards of material and tight corset would allow. With a sigh of relief, she rapped on Tyra's office door.

Tyra opened it quickly.

"I have my dress." Ella held it up. "But if this isn't a good time...."

"It's a perfect time. I was just about to come out and check on you. The office is all yours." She stepped into the hallway. "I also found a large zippered bag our supplier used for shipping the latest batch of tablecloths. It'll do for your dress, at least for now."

"Excellent. Thanks. I'll make this fast."

"Take your time. This gives me a chance to schmoose with old friends." Her stride was brisk as she made tracks for the dining room.

"Okay, Marsh." Ella turned to him.

"I went through the stack and picked the simplest one. No wires." He pulled it out of his pocket and handed it over.

"Exactly what I wanted."

"That's good, because those fancy ones with the structural elements wouldn't have fit in my pocket."

Brit laughed. "Structural elements. Great description."

"They look damned uncomfortable."

"Because they are," Ella said.

"Why would you torture yourself by wearing something like that?"

"We do it for you guys," Faye said. "Sad to say."

"Well, that's—" He cut himself off and glanced at Ella. "That's interesting."

She laughed. "You were gonna say ridiculous, weren't you?"

"No."

"Stupid?"

He grinned. "Yeah, until I realized that would be insulting. Besides, it's none of my business. Your body, your choice. To be honest, I never thought much about the subject until now."

He tipped his hat and backed away. "I'll go request that song."

"Thank you."

As he walked away, Faye sighed. "Why couldn't you fall in love with *him*?"

"Because he's my best friend. I love him as a friend."

"You always say that."

"Because it's true."

"And you've *never* had the urge to turn it into something more?"

Only once. About an hour ago. "If I have, I've killed that urge. Our friendship is precious. I'm not willing to risk losing it."

5

Throwing Stapleton out of Ella's house and roughing him up some had improved Marsh's disposition considerably. Dancing with Ella to a sassy tune would help, too.

He waited until Tequila Toasted ended their number before he approached. They'd started playing here about eight months ago and the Buffalo crowd loved them. Choosing a band to play for Ella's wedding reception had been a no-brainer.

Jeff, lead guitar and vocalist, walked to the edge of the platform and leaned down. "What's up?"

"Ella's changing out of her wedding dress, and then she and I will lead off the dancing."

"I wondered what she planned to do about that. Folks aren't sure about the protocol."

"She didn't think about it, either. It's not like she expected this to happen."

"Yeah. I feel bad for her, but better she found out about the turkey before she married him."

"Right."

"I'll take a wild guess she doesn't want us to play *I Swear*."

"She's requested *Before He Cheats*."

Jeff chuckled. "Perfect. LuAnn does a kick-ass version. Close your eyes and you'll believe we've got Carrie Underwood up here. How long will it take Ella to change?"

"I'd say do one more number. She'll be back by then."

He nodded. "What kind of intro do you want?"

"I've been thinking about it. Maybe just say *please welcome Ella Bradley and Marsh McLintock to the floor.* I don't know what else to say."

"I can work with that."

"We're making this up as we go along. Thanks for being flexible."

"No problem. Hell, we love being encouraged to play our own stuff and the reaction has been great. Only thing is, we don't know if folks like it for dancing or not, since they feel funny about going out on the floor in this situation."

"If it's any consolation, Ella's bridesmaid said she couldn't wait to start dancing to the great music."

"Good to hear." He straightened. "Give me a signal when you're ready for the Carrie Underwood number."

"I'll do that." Turning, he crossed the dance floor in the direction of his mom's table. She was sharing it with Buck and Marybeth — employees who'd become family — and Jess's dad Andy, who'd become family a few months ago.

"Hey, son." She beckoned him over. "Welcome to the granny and grandpa table. How's Ella doing?"

He hunkered down between her chair and Andy's. "She'll be better once she changes out of that dress."

"You brought one from her house just now, didn't you?"

"Yes, ma'am."

His mom's expression softened. "I'm glad you're there for her."

"Which reminds me, Ella and I are going to start off the dancing in a few minutes."

"Great idea." Marybeth beamed at him. "I assume you won't be dancing to *I Swear*."

"No, ma'am."

"I was thinking about that song on the way over here," his mom said. "I made up some new lyrics. *I swear, in case he should show up again, I'll prepare, I swear, I'll give him a knee in the nuts.*"

Andy laughed. "That's clever, Desiree. You should be a writer."

"I've considered it." She winked at Marsh when Andy wasn't looking.

He kept a straight face, but it wasn't easy. Andy was the only one at the table who was clueless about her bestselling Westerns. And she wanted to keep it that way.

"What is the tune you'll dance to?" Marybeth asked.

"You guys should like it. It's appropriate to the occasion."

"You're not gonna tell us, are you?"

He smiled. "It'll be more fun if I don't."

"Okay, a little suspense is good," his mom said. "Speaking of that, do you think Jess will go into labor before the night's over?"

"I have no idea."

"But what's your professional opinion as a doctor? Have you seen any indication that she's about to deliver our eagerly anticipated granddaughter?"

"Sorry, Mom. I can read the signs if I'm looking at a mare, but when it comes to human ladies, I got nuthin'."

"I hope it's tomorrow," Andy said. "That would work out for everyone since it's Sun— oh, there's Ella coming out of the back. I'll bet she's happy to ditch that gargantuan dress."

"She couldn't wait." Marsh rose to his feet and turned. Then he sucked in a breath. In the blue sleeveless dress, Ella still looked like royalty.

She'd carried herself the same way when she'd walked toward center court to accept the state basketball championship trophy ten years ago. She'd been stunning then, and even more so now as she wrested victory from defeat.

Head high, she walked into the main room flanked by Brit and Faye. Her gaze swept the area and came to rest on him. His reaction to that gaze was intense, stirring him in complex ways.

He looked over his shoulder at his mother. "Gotta go."

"I can see that." She wasn't laughing, but she was skating on the edge of it.

Great. Now his mom knew he was in love with Ella. Maybe she'd known it before he did. When it came to her kids, Desiree McLintock didn't just have eyes in the back of her head. She had a three-hundred-and-sixty-degree view.

Crossing the dance floor, he met Ella on the edge of it. "You look terrific."

"Thanks to you, I also feel terrific."

"She wanted to throw away the corset," Faye said. "But I prevailed. It'll be rehomed along with the dress."

Ella sighed. "I still vote for throwing it in the trash. No one should be subjected to that instrument of torture. I'm a new woman without that thing squeezing the breath out of me."

Marsh didn't mean to let his attention stray toward Ella's breasts. It just happened.

She caught him at it and gave him a nudge. "Thank you for saving my tatas."

Dammit, now he was blushing. "You're welcome."

"You're adorable." His grimace made her chuckle. "Sorry, but you are. Is everything set for our dance?"

"As soon as they finish this one, I'll give them the signal, but they probably don't need it. They can see you're back."

"I'm back, baby!" She flashed him a bright smile.

And he lost his heart. Again.

Tequila Toasted wrapped up the tune they'd been playing and got a hearty round of applause.

Jeff acknowledged it with a brief bow. Then he stepped up to the mic. "Thanks for your enthusiastic response to our music, folks. This next number is one you're sure to recognize. Please welcome Ella Bradley and Marsh McLintock as they get this party started!"

With the first chords of the familiar song, the guests clapped and whistled their approval. Marsh spun Ella out on the floor with a fancy two-step they'd perfected over the years. She felt like heaven in his arms. Always had, but tonight was different. He'd faced the truth.

The song's tempo ebbed and flowed, coaxing them to surrender to the seductive rhythm. He held her gaze as they whirled and dipped in response. So easy. So right. She laughed as he executed a complicated move that they'd only tried a few times. She matched him, step for step. Flawless. Tuned in. To him.

The guests rose to their feet, clapping in time and swaying with the music. The song suited his mood. And hers. She was the least violent person in his world, but tonight she was understandably taken by a song of justified revenge.

The need to settle the score had pushed her to hold her reception and choose this song. It had driven him to grab her ex and shove him out of her house.

They'd triumphed, and now he longed to hold her in his arms, and not just on the dance floor. Maybe when he took her home... no, couldn't go there. Ah, but it would be sweet. Wild and sweet.

The song surged into the last chorus and the room crackled with electricity. Ella had never looked more beautiful, her breath coming fast, her cheeks pink with excitement. She'd forgotten all about Stapleton. He'd bet his life on it. If only...

The song eased into the last few bars. And was over. He hugged her tight and she hugged him back as the guests went crazy.

"Thank you, Marsh." Her voice was husky. "You're amazing."

"You, too." And then he had to let her go. They'd done it. They'd put this celebration on track to wipe out the ugliness of the cancelled wedding and the cheating fiancé.

He longed to haul her back into his arms, but he didn't dare. If he did, he'd kiss her. "What now?"

She laughed, clearly riding the wave of energy their dance had stirred up. "Time to drink!"

"Tell me what you want." Friends and family poured onto the dance floor, heading in their direction.

"Something I've never had before. Something strong that looks pretty and tastes great. Surprise me."

"I'll see what I can do. Or what Clint can do." He scanned the crowd and found his brother. Once he got his attention, he pointed toward the antique bar.

Clint nodded and eventually they each navigated a path to it. "Whatcha need, bro?"

"Something strong, pretty and tasty."

"I assume this is a drink we're talking about." He moved to the flip-top, let himself in and came around to face Marsh.

"What else?"

"That's also a perfect description of my ideal woman."

"Come to think of it, mine, too."

Clint surveyed him with a knowing glance. "Uh-huh."

"Cut it out."

Clint moved to the far end of the bar, away from where Brandy was busy handling orders, and beckoned Marsh to follow him. "Look, I work here. I watch couples on the dance floor all the time. I know what I saw."

"Doesn't matter."

"The hell it doesn't. And don't give me that *we're just friends* crap. It could be true for her. I don't know her as well as I know you. You're in love with her so don't bother denying it."

"Okay, I won't bother. I still need that drink."

"A red, white and blue should satisfy your criteria for strong, pretty and tasty." Clint sighed as he grabbed a tall glass from the shelf. "I've always kind of envied you, Marsh, because you're super smart and you're an incredible vet. But I sure don't envy you, now."

"I'm not what she needs. It's just that simple."

"No, it's just that complicated." Clint started mixing the drink. "You're exactly what she needs, but she's convinced herself otherwise. And so have you. You're both trapped in this setup you created when you were too young to know any better. And that sucks."

"When you're right, you're right."

"What if she's stuck, too? What if she's secretly in love with you and doesn't want to say anything?"

"Clint, until a few hours ago, she was in love with Stapleton. For all I know, she still is. She might not want to be, but she had to have cared deeply about the guy if she—"

"You have a point. I hate to admit it, but the timing is terrible. All I ask is that you pay attention. Don't assume this is a one-sided deal."

"She kissed me today."

Clint's head snapped up. "Aha! Did you kiss her back?"

"Not really."

"Oh, for God's sake. You're hopeless." He returned his focus to the drink. "I thought Cheyenne was a mess, but at least he took what Kendall offered. Initially, anyway. After that he pretty much effed it up, but you didn't even—"

"She was stressed, acting out of character. I doubt she'll do it again."

"Maybe, but promise me this, dingbat. If she kisses you again..." Clint pushed the colorful drink across the antique bar. "Kiss her back."

He smiled. "Even a loser like me knows that much. Thanks for the drink."

6

Ella sank into her chair, breathing hard after a vigorous two-step with... what was his name? She glanced at her tablemates — Faye, Brit and Marsh. "Who was that guy?"

"Aaron." Faye looked amused.

"Aaron who?"

"Miller. He works summers for his dad at the hardware store. He's a sophomore at Idaho State."

"No wonder he looks like a kid. I think he's the youngest one I've danced with."

Faye reached over and patted her arm. "You really don't have to dance with all of them, toots."

"Yes, I do. It's a fun challenge. I'm glad I thought of it. First Marsh, then my dad, and then *everybody* else." She flung out her arm to encompass the room.

"I hate to rain on your parade," Faye said, "but even leaving the women out of it, you still don't have enough time to check off all the guys in this room. Figuring in one more break for the band and the line dances everyone loves, it's mathematically impossible."

"Bummer." She sat back, arms crossed.

"Is it really that important, sis?"

"Yes. Each time I dance with someone, I thank them for their kindness in coming to my reception. If they're with someone, I ask them to convey my thanks to their partner or wife."

"What about paying a visit to every table, instead?" Marsh said it gently, as if talking to someone who wasn't quite with the program.

Which she wasn't. Those red, white and blue drinks were powerful. "I thought of that, but this seemed better." And less dangerous. If she dedicated herself to dancing with every man in the room, that left her no time to dance with Marsh.

When the Carrie Underwood tune had ended, she'd wanted to drag him off in a corner and have her way with him. The strong drinks she'd consumed since then had tamed her libido, but she still didn't trust herself to get body-to-body with the guy.

They'd made a solemn promise and he'd never strayed from it. She was the problem and the explanation wasn't tough to find. Her fiancé, *ex-*fiancé, had humiliated her.

In contrast, Marsh had heroically stood by her through the entire episode. He'd put on a show with their dance that had dazzled the guests. And ignited a flame that still flickered, even after three of those red, white and blues.

Should she order one more, which would render her incapable of seducing him? Or try to sober up and count on willpower?

She turned to Marsh. "You're right. Visiting each of the tables is a better plan. I'll get another red, white and blue to sip as I make the rounds. Then maybe it's time to call it a night."

"Good plan." Marsh pushed back his chair, "I'll fetch your drink and make the rounds with you."

Uh-oh. "Thanks, but you don't need to come with me."

"It's no trouble."

She caught a quick glance among her three companions. "You're afraid I'll embarrass myself if I don't have a keeper."

Faye looked her in the eye. "You've been brave and strong ever since leaving the church. Getting smashed is perfectly okay under the circumstances. Just let Marsh tag along and watch out for you. You'll be in safe hands."

She stifled a groan of frustration. Marsh might not be safe, though. Good thing she'd ordered that drink. "I understand." She turned to him. "I appreciate you babysitting me."

He held her gaze "I'm just helping a friend get through a tough time."

Had his lashes always been that long? His brown eyes that expressive? She fought the impulse to grab him by his shirt and kiss him until he couldn't see straight. "Why don't I get started?"

"Okay."

She scooted her chair back. "I'll head over to—" His touch as he helped her up made her forget what she was going to say. Or do.

Hold me. But he didn't. Her best friend was many things, but mind-reader wasn't one of them, thank goodness. Excusing himself from the table, he went to the bar to order her drink.

Faye glanced up at her. "Are you okay?"

"I'm fine." She took a deep breath. "A little tipsy, but I can handle schmoozing the Wenches and the Serving Boys." Two members of Desiree's book club had husbands who'd given themselves that title.

"Or you could wait here until Marsh gets back."

Truth be told, she wasn't exactly steady on her pins. "All right, I probably should. He won't be long." The object of her affections leaned against the bar, chatting with Clint while he waited for her drink. Hours ago he'd ditched his Western jacket and draped it over the back of his chair. He'd hung his hat there, too.

Even without the jacket, his shoulders were a mile wide. Was it her imagination, or had he put on some muscle? Had his butt always been that tight? She'd focused on keeping her distance tonight, but evidently absence had made her heart, and other body parts, grow fonder.

She was used to having Marsh around, so by avoiding him, she might be feeding the very obsession she was trying to tamp down. Maybe if she stayed close, she'd recapture the easy camaraderie they'd had for years. The squiggles in her stomach would go away.

Or they'd get worse. She pressed a hand to her midsection as he came toward her, a drink in his hand and a smile on that beautiful mouth. Her lips tingled as if their brief kiss had happened seconds ago instead of hours.

"Decided to wait for me, huh?"

"I did." Accepting the drink, she took a sip. "Delish. Thank you."

"You're welcome." He picked up his hat. "Ready?"

"I am. See you guys in a bit." But as she walked away from the table, her drink sloshed perilously close to the rim of the glass. "Hang on. I'd better drink some of this so I don't spill it."

He paused. "I'm in no hurry."

She took a couple of swallows, evaluated the level and took another sip. "I'm glad you suggested table-hopping. I haven't talked to the Wenches tonight, and I want to. After all, they gave me that lovely shower. It was so—" She gasped. "Good Lord, the *presents*. I completely forgot about them. I'll give everything back, of course, and—"

"Not tonight."

"Well, no, but maybe I should make an announcement to that effect."

He smiled. "By all means. Everyone knows you're a greedy Gus."

"Oh, stop it. I'm just trying to—"

"Weren't you the one who put a note in the invitation discouraging gifts? That you and Warner had everything you needed?"

"But folks gave us stuff, anyway. And I want them to know I'm not going to keep it."

"Trust me, nobody's worried about that right now." Marsh rested his hands on her shoulders and gazed into her eyes. "The gifts are a problem for another day."

"Tomorrow. I'll start tomorrow."

"Or maybe the next day."

"No, tomorrow. It'll weigh on my mind until it's done."

"Want my help?"

"You know I do, but—"

"Then you've got it." He gave her shoulders a squeeze and let go.

She let out a sigh of regret. Whoops.

As if he'd picked up on it, he tucked an arm around her waist. "Let's go see the Wenches and their Serving Boys."

"Let's do." The Wenches' rainbow-colored dress code made them easy to spot—Colleen in red, Teresa in orange, Nancy in yellow, Cindy in blue and Annette in indigo. They were missing Desiree's purple and Jess's green, since they were seated with the McLintocks tonight.

"I never asked if Beau is a Serving Boy now that Jess is one of the Wenches."

"Yes, he is, and proud of it. But tonight he's a McLintock first and a Serving Boy second."

"Yeah, your mom and Jess's dad aren't letting that pregnant couple stray far from their sight. First grandchild. That's a big deal."

"Sure is." He guided her between the tables toward the boisterous two-table arrangement occupied by the Wenches.

How did he feel about kids? In all the deep discussions they'd had over the years, they'd never talked about it. "Do you want children?"

"In a general sense, yes. But I could fall in love with someone who can't have them or has reasons not to want them. If she's the one, the kid thing is not a deal breaker."

"That's a great answer." And what a lucky lady to have Marsh McLintock as her life partner.

"How about you?"

"Warner and I— but it doesn't matter anymore what Warner and I decided, does it?"

His grip tightened at her waist. "Nope."

"Here come Ginger and Fred!" Nancy beckoned them over.

Marsh laughed. "If my mom hadn't shown us old movies every afternoon after school, I probably wouldn't get that reference."

"That's why I got off the bus at his place," Ella said, "Snacks, movies and TV reruns. I still love those old-timey musicals."

"You must have picked up some tips," Nancy said, "because you two are spectacular on the dance floor."

"Thank you." Ella smiled at her. "It was fun." And had inspired ideas she had no business having. "Anyway, before I pack it in, I want to thank you all for your kindness in showing up at my no-wedding reception."

"We had to come." Cindy's teal hair matched a subtle stripe in her cobalt dress while also honoring Ella's wedding color. "It gives us a chance to hatch our revenge plot."

"Like cancelling your insurance policies with Warner?"

Teresa waved her hand in a dismissive gesture. "That's a done deal but it lacks drama. We're looking for visible payback."

"Visible?"

George, Colleen's husband, looked up at Ella. "After what I've heard tonight, I'm never making these ladies mad. They're brutal."

"Now, George." Colleen patted his arm. "We're not going to physically harm this worthless piece of garbage."

"He'll emerge without a scratch on him," Annette said.

"Unless he tries to hide in the bushes." Nancy flashed her evil villain smile. "We can't be responsible if he dives into a thorny—"

"Why would he dive into a bush?" Ella didn't get it, but then she wasn't firing on all cylinders.

"Obviously he'll be naked," Annette said.

Ella stared at the most reserved member of the group. Usually. But tonight her flushed cheeks told a different story. She was well and truly ticked. "Why would he be naked?"

"That's one teensy detail we haven't worked out," Teresa said. "In a plan yet to be finalized, we'll strand him naked at the edge of town with no option but to walk home that way."

Ella finished off her drink. "Sounds fine to me, but what if he brings charges against you? Assuming he can prove it was you."

"If we do it right," Nancy said, "he'll be too embarrassed to bring charges."

"Okay, then." She glanced at Marsh. "We should leave them to it."

"Absolutely." He tipped his hat. "Happy plotting." He steered Ella away from the table. "You never heard any of that."

"Even if I did, I'm under the influence so my testimony would be worthless. I'm not so sure about you, though. You stopped drinking an hour ago."

"I'm counting on my mom."

"To get you out of testifying?"

"To stop them from doing something that could get them arrested." He paused. "Where to?"

"You know what?" She looked at her empty glass. "It's time. Let's scoop up Brit and Faye and head out."

"Done." He tucked her in close as they worked their way back to the table. "Ella's ready to leave. So if you're both—"

"We thought we were," Faye said, "but while you were gone, we got our second wind. You go ahead. We can easily find a way home."

Ella blinked. "Oh. Well—" She'd be riding home alone with Marsh? Then again, she was suddenly so tired she could barely stay upright, let alone put the moves on him. "I guess I'll see you guys later, then."

"Text me when you wake up, sis. Tomorrow's Sunday, so I didn't have anything planned. We could hang out."

"I'd be up for that," Brit said. "Give me a shout, too."

"Sounds good. It might be noon, though."

Faye waved a hand. "No worries. Like I said, I'll be around."

"Me, too," Brit smiled. "Get some sleep, girlfriend."

"I feel like I could sleep for a week." She leaned down and gave them each a quick hug and grabbed her purse off the back of her chair. "See you tomorrow." The she turned to Marsh. "We're outta here."

7

Marsh slid one arm around a clearly exhausted Ella and hooked his jacket over his shoulder. The minute they stepped outside, she shivered. "Take this." He draped his jacket around her.

"Thank you." She tugged the lapels closed and let out a sigh.

"Want to put it on?"

"This is fine. How far is the truck?"

"Not too far. I was lucky." Tucking her in close, he started off. She must be really wiped out if she took his jacket without protest and was worried about how far they had to walk. "I'm glad you didn't change your mind and decide to stay."

"Honestly, I don't think I could have managed another five minutes. I didn't sleep much last night."

"That makes two of us."

"You? The guy who's famous for being able to zonk out no matter what?"

"I wanted your big day to be perfect. His gonzo plan of flying in this morning set us up for failure, but there wasn't a damn thing I could do about it."

"My fault. I fell for his story that finalizing this deal would put us closer to having a down payment for a house."

"Do you think there ever was such a deal?"

Her laugh was bitter. "No. Why was I so gullible?"

"You were in love. You wanted him to be for real."

"I did." She fell silent.

He gave her shoulder a squeeze. "The truck's at the end of the block, across the street. We're almost there."

"I'll turn twenty-nine this year."

Odd comment. "Me, too. So what?"

"Before you know it, I'll be past the recommended age to have babies."

The sudden ache of longing took him by surprise. It burrowed deep. Something new to contend with.

"Beau and Jess's baby shower was a wake-up call for me. Warner had dropped hints about getting married, and when he said he could hardly wait to have kids...."

Marsh clenched his jaw. The bastard had capitalized on her yearning for motherhood. What a prince. "Well, damn him to hell for lousing up your dream. I'm sorry."

"He was eager to get a head start by ditching birth control as soon as we were engaged."

His world tilted. "Are you saying you might be—"

"Nope. I insisted on waiting until we were closer to the wedding."

Whew. "Then he went to Florida."

"Thank God! Or I could be married to him *and* pregnant with his child." She shuddered. "Although he wouldn't have met Dinah."

Marsh braced himself. Was she about to convince herself Warner was a victim of circumstance?

"And I'd have no clue I was married to a liar and a cheat."

He let out a sigh of relief.

"Don't worry, Marsh. I saw what I wanted to see before, but now my vision's twenty-twenty."

"Good." He checked to make sure no one was coming down the street before they crossed it.

"You never did like him, did you?"

"I tried to, but—"

"I was pretty sure you didn't like him, but I put it down to jealousy."

"Jealousy?" Was she on to him?

"If I get married, we can't hang out as much."

He relaxed. "I like to think I could handle that." He opened the passenger door and helped her in.

"Thanks. I appreciate the hand up since I'm toasted. But we don't need to make a habit of me needing to be helped into your truck."

"If you say so."

"Want your coat back?"

"Why don't you keep it for now?" He closed the door and rounded the hood. Had jealousy played a part in his dislike of Stapleton? Maybe a little. The jerk hadn't been good enough for her. But none of the guys she'd dated had measured up.

Even he didn't deserve someone as wonderful as Ella.

He climbed behind the wheel, buckled up and glanced over at her. She was busy pulling the pins from her updo and dropping them in her purse. "Fasten your—"

"Oh. Right." She snapped the tongue into the groove and continued deconstructing her hairstyle. Golden waves fell to her shoulders. "Full disclosure, I was jealous of Sabrina."

"You were?" Mesmerized by the transformation when she took down her hair, he hadn't managed to put the key in the ignition. He remedied that.

"I thought you were going to marry her, which meant I wouldn't see you as much."

"She took the job in Boston before I could pop the question." He turned the key and the engine rumbled.

"You loved her, though. I could tell."

"Not enough to give up everything here and move to Boston." Backing out of the spot, he pointed the truck toward her house.

"Did you ask her to consider staying?"

"Nope." He put on the brakes at the town's only stoplight. "The way I look at it, you should be willing to die for the person you're marrying. I wasn't even willing to move to Boston. Clearly she wasn't the love of my life."

"Huh."

"What?" The light turned and he stepped on the gas.

"I wish you'd said that thing about dying while we were making arrangements for the wedding."

"No reason to. Just because it's my criteria doesn't mean—"

"But it's a good test. I can't picture myself taking a bullet for Warner."

"Well, not now, obviously, but before, when you didn't know that he was a piece of—"

"Even then." She covered a yawn and leaned back against the seat. "I don't think I would have."

"You'd know better than me."

"There are several people I'd take a bullet for. He's not one of them." She snuggled down, burrowing into his jacket. "This is cozy. Most relaxed I've felt since… May."

"Want some music?"

"Sure."

He punched a button and turned down the volume. Lonestar's *Amazed* came on.

"Nice." Ella rested her head against the seat and looked over at him, her eyelids drooping. "Thanks, Marsh."

"You're welcome." He focused on the road again. The music rolled over him, easing any remaining tension. "I wasn't kidding about helping you with the gifts."

No response.

He checked on her. Just that fast she was out, lulled to sleep by booze, the purr of the engine and Lonestar on the radio.

Another two blocks and he was in sight of her bungalow. He took his foot off the gas and coasted, rolling along the street at a snail's pace. Stapleton didn't have a key anymore, but that didn't rule out breaking and entering. At this point, anything was possible with that asswipe.

Normally Marsh wasn't in favor of revenge plots, but Stapleton needed to leave town. As deluded as he was, he might resist the idea. The Wenches' plan might be too dicey, but if they could figure out a way to coax him out the door, they'd be doing everyone a public service.

The driveway was clear, so Marsh drove in and cut the motor. Ella didn't wake up. He flipped the switch so the dome light wouldn't come on, climbed out and locked the truck. Her place looked quiet, but he wasn't taking any chances.

Letting himself into her house, he scanned the shadows in the living room. Nothing out of place. Not a sound. But he was his mother's son, gifted with a vivid imagination. He searched the house, including the closets and the shower, before he was satisfied that Stapleton wasn't hiding in wait.

For good measure he made one more pass, taking time to pull back the covers on her bed. Then he checked the locks on every window and the back door deadbolt. All secure.

He left the lights off and the front door open as he walked out to the porch. He knew her house almost as well as his own and the faint light provided by a half-moon and the soft glow of her front porch lamp were enough.

Opening the passenger door with care, he pocketed his keys and unbuckled the seat belt. He'd been through this routine before, once after a New

Year's Eve party at Rowdy Ranch and again when she'd fallen asleep on his couch while they were binge-watching *Maverick* reruns.

He hooked one arm behind her knees and slid the other under her shoulder blades. His jacket fell away as he lifted her gently and backed away from the truck. She reacted like a sleepy child, resting her head on his shoulder and wrapping her arms around his neck. He carried her toward the porch.

She felt lighter this time. Yeah, he was also stronger, but he wouldn't be surprised if she'd lost weight while under the stress of planning a wedding in three short months. He'd lobbied for a Christmas ceremony, but she'd been adamant about doing it before school started.

Now that she'd confided her sense of urgency about having kids, the timing made more sense. He could father a child into his dotage. Ella's time to conceive, while it still could be measured in years, was limited. Given that, he could understand.

He walked slowly, partly because he didn't want to wake her up and partly because he loved holding her. Her warmth and her sweet aroma weren't always this close. Friendly hugs happened, but not as often as he'd like.

He'd told himself that their dancing was about mind-challenging steps and aerobic exercise. Nope. Dancing allowed him to touch, hold and breathe in Ella Bradley for the length of a country song.

How long had he been kidding himself that his feelings were platonic? Longer than he cared to admit. But she'd shown no signs of wanting to change the status quo.

The porch steps put his abs to the test. and he blessed the weight bench in his spare bedroom and the punching bag on the back porch. Ella was fit but she wasn't tiny by any means. She was almost tall enough to look him in the eye.

And didn't he love it when she did? Her expressive blue gaze could exasperate him one minute and send him into helpless laughter the next. Hanging out with Ella was never boring.

He turned sideways to get through the doorway without hitting her feet against the frame. She'd lost a shoe. Oh, well. He'd have to go back for her purse, so he'd look for her shoe along the way.

Nudging the door closed with the toe of his boot, he walked through the living room. One more doorway to navigate. Done. He laid her gently on the bed and had to unhook her arms from around his neck.

She murmured a sleepy protest.

He pitched his voice low. "Let go, Ella."

When she obediently loosened her grip, her arms fell limply to her sides, and that didn't wake her, either. One more step to go.

The first time he'd carried her in here after she'd fallen asleep on him, he'd stripped her down to her underwear so she'd be more comfortable. The next day, instead of being embarrassed he'd done that, she'd thanked him for not leaving her to get tangled up in her clothes during the night.

Might as well follow the same program as the other two times. He slipped off her shoe and her toenails reflected what little light was in the room.

She'd talked about painting them gold so maybe she had.

That left only her dress. She offered no resistance when he turned her on her side to access the back zipper. Her deep sleep made her vulnerable, though, and that worried him. He'd leave the house locked up tight, but a determined man would find a way in.

He eased her to her back and worked the dress down over her arms, her hips, and finally her feet. Her comfy bra looked better on her than in the drawer.

Better shift his attention before he landed in creepy ogling territory. Her panties looked like they were made from the same soft cotton. Non-binding. He pulled the covers up, draped her dress over a chair in the corner and left the room.

As he stepped out on the porch again, an SUV disappeared around the corner. Stapleton would have switched to his own vehicle by now. Marsh couldn't say that SUV was his, but he couldn't say it wasn't, either.

He located Ella's missing shoe on the bottom step and went to fetch her purse. Right where she left it on the floor of the truck. Her keys were in the pocket where she kept them. All her keys. He took the time to check.

Was he getting paranoid? Maybe. But Stapleton had thought invading her living room and drinking her beer was a stellar idea. He had no respect for the woman he'd planned to marry or the one he'd bedded in Florida.

In Marsh's estimation, that made him a menace, especially when Ella was down for the count. He couldn't leave her alone. Grabbing his jacket, he locked the truck and headed inside.

Should he take the couch? Except he was short on sleep, too. If Stapleton gained entry through the back of the house, he might get to Ella before Marsh did.

He locked the front door and hung her purse on the hook where she liked to keep it. He put his jacket and hat on the next hook. Taking off his boots and belt, he tucked the belt into the boots and set them by the front door before returning to her bedroom.

She was right where he'd left her, which gave him plenty of room on the other side of the bed. That stationed him between Ella and the door. Fully clothed, he stretched out on top of the covers and was asleep in seconds.

_8_

Ella was in a church, but it didn't look like Wagon Train's quaint white clapboard one. More like some giant cathedral. It was empty except for her, Warner and a priest in elaborate robes at the end of the aisle.

She had on her bulky wedding dress, which made it impossible to get away from Warner. He had her by the arm as he dragged her down the aisle toward the priest waiting to perform the ceremony.

No! She tried to cry out but couldn't make a sound. *No, no, no!* She balled up her fist and tried to smack Warner in the head. He caught her wrist.

"Ella, wake up."

Marsh's voice. Why was Warner talking in Marsh's voice?

She called his name, but it came out garbled.

"Ella, it's me. Marsh. You're having a nightmare. Wake up."

She fought her way to the surface, opened her eyes and let out a yelp. Marsh's face was inches from hers. "What are you doing here?"

"You fell asleep in the truck, so I—"

"Right." The fog cleared. "You brought me home. You turned on the radio. They were playing *Amazing.* That's the last thing I remember."

"I carried you in and... got you ready for bed."

She touched the cotton of her comfy bra and smiled. "Thank you. Be glad you didn't have to pry me out of that corset."

"No kidding. The blue dress was easy to get off, though. I left it on the back of your chair."

"Thank you. I love that dress."

"Looks good on you, too." He smothered a yawn. "Matches your eyes."

She gazed at him. "You still haven't told me why you're here. Is your truck battery dead?"

"Truck runs fine. I decided... well, you were really conked out, and even though I made sure the doors and windows are all locked, I...."

"Warner."

"He probably wouldn't try anything, but even so, I—"

"That was my nightmare. He was dragging me down the aisle of an empty cathedral and I couldn't fight him off because of that damned wedding dress."

"I'm glad I was here, then. It's no fun to wake up from a nightmare when you're by yourself."

"No. This was way better." She peered at him. His beard darkened his jaw and his hair was all mussed. Cute as hell. "You must be more worried than you let on if you decided to stay. Not only that, but you're right here, between me and the door."

"Like I said, I don't really expect him to be that stupid, but just in case, I—"

"Oh, no." Panic gripped her again. "He has a key."

"Not anymore."

"Why not?"

"I have it."

"How did you get it?"

He went silent.

"Marsh? How did you get that key away from him?"

"It doesn't matter. Just accept that I—"

"Oh, no, you don't." She sat up. "There's a story here and you're going to tell it."

He propped his head on his hand. "It's no big deal." His gaze flicked to the clock on her nightstand. "It's after three-sixteen in the morning. You should get some more sleep. We both should."

She studied him. "I don't believe you know any slight-of-hand tricks, and you've been with me ever since we left the church, except... except when you came to get my bra and my dress!"

"Ella, leave it be."

"Did you go to his house, force your way in and demand the key? Did you beat him up, after all?"

"None of the above."

"'You know I'll pester you until you tell me, so you might as well spill the beans and save us both some time."

He sighed. "When I came to get your dress and bra, he was here."

"In my *bed*?"

"In your living room, asleep on your couch. You're missing three beers, by the way."

"He came here? I can't believe he did that. Why would he do that?"

"He figured you'd come home eventually and the two of you would talk everything out and make amends."

"He's crazy."

"A little bit, yeah. Anyway, I let myself in quietly and found him asleep. Your key was lying on the coffee table, so I put it in my pocket."

"Good man. Then what?"

"I woke him up and convinced him to leave."

"And he just walked out?"

"Not exactly."

"You threw him out, didn't you?"

He shrugged. "More or less."

"You did. I wish I'd been there. I would have loved to see that. Thank you."

"It wasn't like I could let him stay and continue to stink up your place."

"You weren't going to tell me, were you?"

"Not unless I had to. But now that I think about it, you need to know he doesn't have a key anymore. That should make you feel safer."

"You must not think I'm very safe if you chose to guard me through the night."

"Maybe I'm overreacting."

"He's not a nice man."

"No."

Anxiety ate at the calm she so longed for. "I have a thought, but feel free to say no. It's a huge imposition."

"No such thing where you're concerned."

"You haven't heard my idea yet."

"So lay it on me."

"I want to stay at your place for the next few days, until the dust settles and I'm not afraid to sleep in my own bed."

"Done."

"You're sure?"

"If you hadn't suggested it, I would have. You'll be safe out at the ranch. He wouldn't dare show up there. He's already afraid of me, and my brothers will add to the fear factor for a guy like Stapleton."

"Did you beat him up? You can tell me. I won't tell any—"

"I didn't beat him up. His exit wasn't exactly painless, but it was bloodless. I told him not to come near you ever again, but unless I shadow you twenty-four-seven, I can't make that stick. I'd feel a whole lot better if you're out at Rowdy Ranch for the next little while."

"Good, then it's settled. Let's go now."

His eyes widened. "Now?"

"After this discussion I'll never get back to sleep. I'll pack up my truck and follow you out there."

"Let's not take your truck." He sat up and swung his feet to the floor.

"Why not? I might need to go somewhere."

"Somewhere you could run into Warner?"

She let out a breath. "I guess that's a possibility. Staying out at the ranch for a while is the best option. I'll just leave my truck in the garage, then."

"We might as well take all your wedding gifts while we're at it. I can load them while you're getting ready if you'll tell me where to look."

"Great idea." She climbed out of bed and turned on the lamp on the nightstand. "The kitchen gadgets, dishes and glassware are in the pantry in the boxes they came in. I decided not to use anything until Warner and I—" She took a deep breath. "Anyway, that should make it easy if you'd be willing to haul those out to the truck. Same thing with the linens. They're in my linen closet in their original zippered bags."

"I'll get on it." He headed for the door.

"Marsh?"

"What?" He turned around. Then he focused on a point somewhere over her head.

Why wasn't he looking at her? "Thank you for agreeing to this."

"You're welcome." He left quickly.

Good grief, was he uncomfortable seeing her in her bra and panties? That made no sense. It wasn't like he'd never been privy to the view before.

Besides, she'd gone swimming with him more times than she could count. Her cotton underwear wasn't nearly as sexy as her bathing suits, especially the bikini. But something had him spooked.

Maybe he'd picked up on her lustful feelings for him. Oh, God, what if she'd talked in her sleep? According to Faye and Brit, she did that sometimes. No telling what she might have said after an evening of struggling with her libido. How embarrassing if he'd been treated to an erotic monologue he was desperately trying to forget.

She dressed quickly in jeans, running shoes and a sweatshirt. Then she pulled out a suitcase and packed enough clothes to get her through the next few days. Her toiletries went in an overnight bag.

By the time she carried both out to the porch, Marsh was tucking an armful of new sheets and towels into the back seat. She walked over. "Did you get the quilt Teresa made? I showed you that, right?"

"Is it blue and green?"

"That's the one."

"It wasn't wrapped. My truck's clean, but—"

"You're right. I'll find something to put it in." She set down her suitcase and overnight bag. "I doubt she'll take it back, but I'd like to keep it with the other gifts so I remember to discuss it with her."

"I think I got everything else. It helped that you left it all packaged up."

She glanced into the back seat piled high with boxes and zippered bags. "Doesn't look like you have room for my suitcase."

"It'll fit in the back. I checked to make sure before I filled up the seat."

"Then I'll get the quilt and close up the house. I won't be long."

"I'll stow your suitcase and warm up the cab."

"Great." The breeze was chilly, but she'd been so focused on making her getaway that she hadn't noticed. Hurrying into the house, she bagged up the quilt and turned off the lights.

Her purse hung in its spot by the door. Marsh must have put it there. Such a good guy. Such a thoughtful friend. She would *not* mess up a relationship they'd taken more than twenty years to build.

Purse over her shoulder and the bagged quilt tucked under her arm, she locked up and walked across the yard to Marsh's truck.

He got out and opened the back door. "I'll take it. I rearranged things to make room."

"It's my favorite wedding gift. I'm sure this quilt took her hours."

"And she enjoyed every minute. She loves to quilt." He tucked it in and closed the door. Then he started around the back of the truck.

"Marsh."

He paused and turned back. "What?"

"I'll get myself in."

"Okay." He shrugged. "I had to put your overnight case on the floor by your feet."

"That's fine. It's not as bad as that wedding dress." She hurried around the truck, hopped in and shut the door.

Now that she was truly awake, the faint scent of Marsh's spicy cologne sparked subtle echoes of emotions he'd stirred up on the dance floor. An aroma of vibrant male added to the sensual tug.

The radio came on when he turned the key and Tim McGraw filled the silence with *It's Your Love*. Not helping. "Could we please turn that off?"

"Oh, sure." He punched the button and backed out of the drive. "Was that one of the songs you and—"

"No. We never had a certain song. He wasn't into that."

Marsh said something under his breath.

"What?"

"Never mind. Not important."

"You're wondering what a sentimental sap like me was doing with a guy who didn't care if we had a special song."

"More or less. Cruder language."

She smiled. "Let's just agree that I made a bad choice and leave it at that."

"Fine with me."

"But I would like to talk about something."

"You bet." He leaned against the seat and straightened his arms, pushing against the steering wheel as if he needed to stretch out the kinks. "Shoot."

"A while ago, when we were in my bedroom and I turned on the light, I sensed some weirdness. Since you've seen me in my undies before, I wonder if I've said or done anything to cause you to be uncomfortable."

"No, ma'am." His answer came quickly. Too quickly.

She sucked in air and took the plunge. "I've been known to talk in my sleep. Tell me honestly, did I do that? Did I say anything inappropriate to you tonight?"

"You did not." But he was clearly agitated.

"Okay, Marsh. What's going on with you?"

9

Marsh scrambled for an answer. Clint had told him to pay attention to Ella's behavior, and clearly she wasn't overcome with desire. He was still good ol' Marsh, her best friend who should be unmoved by seeing her in her underwear.

He cleared his throat. "I think..." There was the problem. He couldn't think. The image of Ella standing beside her bed in the lamplight, wearing only a skimpy bra and panties, her hair tousled as if she'd been having wild sex— how was he supposed to be immune to that? "It's been a stressful time."

"I would agree with you."

"Under normal circumstances, I'd look at you and see my best friend. But after all this drama, after imagining you married to that scumbag and potentially ending up pregnant with his child, I'm more aware of you as a... woman."

"You didn't see me that way before?" She sounded insulted.

"Of course, but in a general way."

"General? I'm not sure I like that, either. I'm not some vague representation of a female human being."

"I don't mean it like that." He was in the weeds. No way out around it. "I didn't picture you having sex."

"And now you do?"

"No! I mean I realize that you could, that you do, that you— oh, hell. When you climbed out of bed in your bra and panties, all mussed and adorable, I had a... problem."

"An erection?"

"Not a full-blown one because I was fighting it, but I couldn't spend any more time looking at you, which is where the weirdness came from."

"Oh. Is it a mistake for me to stay with you?"

"Absolutely not. I can—"

"Because maybe your sister would be willing to have me bunk with her. Or your mom, although she always has so much to do that I hate to suggest—"

"You're staying with me. We've known each other forever. It'll be fine." *Just keep telling yourself that, dude.*

"It's true I know you better than any other member of your family, but if having me around has the potential to give you a—"

"It won't. You'll be wearing clothes."

"I was wearing clothes tonight."

"More clothes. I doubt you wander around the house naked, or even semi-naked."

"Marsh, let's put our cards on the table."

Let's not. "Okay."

"Are you saying that now my body turns you on?"

"Under certain circumstances."

"Like when I'm wearing nothing but my undies?"

"That would be one of the circumstances."

"Then I promise I won't come out of your spare room wearing only my undies."

"About that. I was planning to give you my room and take the Murphy bed in the spare room."

"Not happening. I won't let you put yourself out."

"I've set up my weight bench in the spare room and I use it every day around six in the morning."

"Six? Really?"

"Really. So you see, putting you in my room will be better for both of us. You can have the adjoining bathroom and I'll take the one in the hall." Then he wouldn't run into her when she was heading to the shower wearing only a robe. Did she pack one? Sweat trickled down his spine. He turned the heater down.

"If I'd known you'd be giving up your bed and your bathroom, I wouldn't have suggested this. I didn't know the spare room was your workout space."

"I just got the bench in May. You've been a little preoccupied this summer." And they were on safer ground. Instead of discussing his reaction to her body, they were negotiating their shared space.

"I feel like I've been under a spell this summer. All I could think about was getting married and having kids."

"No wonder, after all the excitement about Maverick. Stapleton took advantage of that to lock you into the program."

"If it makes you feel any better, the spell is broken."

"I do feel better. But I thought about what you said, and it's valid. It doesn't mean you have to have kids immediately, though."

"I know. I panicked and almost landed in a very bad place."

"Wish I'd known you were freaking out about the baby thing."

"Nobody knew. Well, except Warner. I was probably afraid if I discussed it with anyone — you, my mom, Faye, Brit — at least one of you would ask me if I was marrying Warner just so I could start having kids." She sighed. "Which I was, although I couldn't admit it, not even to myself."

"But you must have loved him. You're not that cold and calculating."

"I told myself I loved him, but if I really did, I should have been willing to take a bullet for him, like you said. And I should be heartbroken right now."

"Maybe you are and you're determined to be strong and not show it. You drank a lot of booze at the party. That's something heartbroken folks do."

"It's also something angry folks do." She glanced over at him. "Maybe I'll get to the grief-stricken stage, but right now I'm furious."

"I also have a punching bag."

"For real?"

He laughed. "Guess I should have mentioned that earlier. Didn't know it would be the main attraction."

"When did you get a punching bag?"

"I...um...bought it in May, too."

"I see. Could it be you had some issues to work out about the same time I became engaged to Warner?"

"It's possible."

"You hated him from the get-go, didn't you?"

He smiled. "I don't hate anybody."

"How about intensely dislike?"

"That works."

"And yet you threw yourself into the preparations for my wedding."

"You were running yourself ragged and he was about as much help as a wart on the backside of a mule."

She giggled. "Good one."

"I have more."

"How many?"

"A bunch. I would have trotted them out at the party for your amusement, but for some reason you avoided me all night."

"Yes, I did, and I apologize for that."

"Care to tell me why?"

She hesitated. "It's kind of embarrassing."

"Fair is fair. I told you why I had to get out of your bedroom ASAP."

"Yeah, okay." She took a deep breath. "Remember when I kissed you?"

"Yes." Like he'd ever forget it while he was still living.

"Well, it's sort of like you seeing me differently after all the talk about getting pregnant and stuff. As you said, it was a stressful time, and you were being so heroic and so… manly. I had a little buzz going. That's why I kissed you."

His pulse rate picked up. "I wondered."

"Then you continued to be the man of the hour by fetching my dress and bra. Once I got rid of that dress and corset, I felt giddy. And to top it off, our dance was… spectacular."

"Yes, ma'am." He focused on the road. And breathing.

"That dance turned me on."

His breath hitched and he turned it into a cough. *Me, too.* But he'd be a fool to say it until he found out where she was going with this.

"Don't worry, Marsh. I won't let some random urge ruin our special relationship. You're my best friend in the world. I want to keep it that way."

There was his answer. Friends forever, lovers never.

"Consequently, I decided to play it safe and avoid you until I cooled down."

While knocking back several drinks? Maybe Stapleton wasn't her only motivation for getting smashed.

Now what? They'd each admitted to temporary feelings of lust. Except she didn't know all of it. She didn't know he was in love up to his neck.

He'd always loved her as a friend. But the difference between loving her and being *in* love with her was like the difference between icicles hanging from his front porch and Glacier National Park.

"You're awfully quiet over there. Have I scared the living daylights out of you?"

"Not at all." He sucked in a breath. "It's good we got all this out in the open."

"That's what friends do. That is, if they cherish the friendship. Like the time you teased me about my haircut and hurt my feelings."

"Because I was an idiot."

"Not a complete idiot, because when I told you I didn't appreciate those comments, you apologized. Some people would have accused me of being too sensitive."

"Some people are mean as hell."

"But not you. Which is why I love you."

"I love you, too." The words came out a little huskier than he would have liked, but he was doing the best he could. They'd been saying *I love you* to each other for years. But tonight, for him at least, it meant more. So much more.

_10_

Although the conversation had taken an unexpected direction, Ella was happy with how it had turned out. Judging from Marsh's response to her confession of temporary lust, he wasn't worried that she'd blow up their friendly relationship.

She wouldn't give him any reason to be worried, either. If sharing his house gave her sexual cravings, she'd take it out on the punching bag.

Maybe. He hadn't exactly said she could use it. "Are you willing to share your punching bag while I'm here?"

"Absolutely. That's why I mentioned it. Great stress reliever."

"I've always wanted one."

"Then this is a good chance to try it out for a few days. See if you like it."

"I just realized I don't have gloves, though. Yours won't fit me."

"Angie likes to come over and use the bag and she keeps her gloves at my place. You could ask her if you can borrow 'em."

"I will. I'm loving this punching bag idea. I didn't think to bring my exercise mat and I'll need some physical exercise while I'm out here."

"We could ride tomorrow if you want. I take Sundays off unless someone has an emergency."

"I hate to tell you, but it's already tomorrow."

"So it is. We'll probably need some shuteye before we take that ride. The point is I'll be available to do stuff, but I have a tight schedule next week."

"It's not your duty to keep me entertained, especially since I invited myself. And by the way, Ill pitch in on things like cooking and cleaning. I'll be your roommate, not your houseguest."

He looked over at her. "Hard to believe that in all the years we've been friends, we've never slept under the same roof."

"We almost did when we binge-watched *Maverick.*"

"Guess so." He returned his attention to the road. "I could have brought you a blanket and left you on the couch. Never occurred to me. I just automatically took you home."

"Waking up in the same house is gonna be... different."

"Yes, ma'am."

Awareness made her tingle in places she was trying to forget. Time to change the subject. "I'd love to take that ride today, but don't worry that I'll be stuck with nothing to do while you're working. I brought my laptop. I wasn't going to start on my fall lesson plans yet, but since the honeymoon is DOA, I—"

"Oh, damn. I forgot about your honeymoon. Is any of it refundable?"

"No, but it won't go down the drain."

"Why not?"

"While you were picking up my dress and throwing Warner out of my house, my parents grabbed their phones and worked out a deal with the airline and the B&B. The trip's been moved to my fall break."

"Didn't Stapleton pay for that trip?"

"Nope. My folks did. A wedding present."

"Oh, right. I forgot. It's nice that you'll get to enjoy it, after all."

"And so will you, if you want."

"Me?"

"You don't have to, but when they cancelled Warner's plane ticket they asked who they should book in his place and I said you."

"Not Faye? Or Brit?"

"I thought of them, but they weren't here this summer to help with the wedding. You were. You worked hard. If you don't want to, that's okay, but I thought—"

"Are you kidding? I saw that brochure. I'd be crazy to say no. The place looks awesome."

"See? I knew you'd be excited. We'll have a blast. Way more fun than I would have had with Warner. He was afraid of ziplining and the kayaking scared him, too."

"Scares me a little."

"Same here, but that tells me I need to try it. Warner sounded like he was gonna wimp out."

"If you're doing it, I'm doing it."

She smiled. "Sounds familiar."

"Story of my life. My mom once asked me if I'd jump off a roof just because you did."

"Was that before or after we did it?"

"After. I could say no with a clear conscience because damned if I'd do it *again*."

"I admit the couch cushions didn't work very well. If we could've pulled the mattress off my bed without getting caught, it would have been way better."

"Face it. We're lucky we haven't killed ourselves."

"But think of all the adventures we've had just because you couldn't let me get the best of you."

"You say adventures. I say near-death experiences. Kayaking and ziplining will be a breeze compared to the pie-eating contest."

"Oh, stop it." She punched him lightly on the shoulder. Solid muscle under that shirt. His weight bench and punching bag had yielded results. "You cherished your trophy."

"The bellyache lasted for three days."

"But the trophy changed your life."

"No, it didn't. You like to think so, but—"

"It did! That trophy fanned the flames of your competitive spirit. That's why you became the home-run king of Wagon Train High."

"Wrong. I hit all those homers because I practiced like I was Rocky Balboa. The contest had nothing to do with—"

"Did so."

"Did not."

She caught the dent in his cheek that meant he was smiling. They'd argued this point endlessly. He'd been a decent baseball player, but the summer after he'd won the pie-eating contest, he'd become a star.

After graduation, he'd decided against a baseball scholarship in favor of concentrating on equine medicine. Right choice. He was meant to work with horses.

But she'd never regretted goading him into that pie-eating competition. Winning it had brought out a side of him she cherished. When an occasion called for a dramatic response, he could bring it. Like on the dance floor at the reception. Or when Warner had invaded her house.

Warner. She shivered. He'd made himself at home as if he still had the right to be there. Creepy. Give her a physical challenge and she was ready to tackle it. But interacting with delusional people made her skin crawl.

When Marsh pulled up next to his sturdy log cabin, she sighed in relief. "Thank you for letting me hide out here for a few days."

"It's the only thing that makes sense to me. At least while Stapleton's still a loose cannon." He opened his door. "I'll get your suitcase out of the back, but how about unloading everything else later?"

"Sure." She picked up her overnight case and slung her purse over her shoulder. "I'm going to grab the quilt from the back seat, though. Wrapping up in it will make me feel better and I think Teresa would tell me to go ahead."

"I agree. I'll get the quilt and your suitcase. You can go on in. Door's open."

She climbed down and rounded the cab. "I'll wait for you. I haven't been out here in so long I forgot you leave your door open."

"Not tonight." Handing her the bagged quilt, he closed the door. "Just didn't want you to feel nervous."

"Thanks."

"He won't come to the ranch, though." He walked around to the tailgate, fetched her suitcase, and locked the truck.

"I don't think so, either." She fell into step beside him as they headed for the porch. "If he figures out I'm not home, he'll probably think I'm with my folks. He wouldn't dare go to their house. Not after my mom gave him the evil eye and warned him not to cross paths with my dad."

"Which brings up another point. You'd be safe with them, too. I was so focused on this plan that I honestly didn't think of—"

"In the moment, neither did I. But the truth is, I'd rather be here." She climbed the steps, her feet hitting the treads in time with his.

Whether he matched his stride to hers or vice versa was anybody's guess. Over the years their established patterns had become subconscious. Until now. Like it or not, she'd become hyper aware of every move he made.

"I can't cook like your mom, Ella."

"Neither can I."

He grinned. "Now you tell me."

"You know I can't, smartass. I'll admit her comfort food sounds good after all this drama."

"Are you sure you don't want me to take you over there tomorrow?"

"I'm sure. They'd welcome me with open arms. Then they'd hover. They wouldn't mean to, but they can't help it. They hate seeing their kids unhappy."

"My mom's the same." Shifting her suitcase to his left hand, he opened the door for her.

She stepped into the dark living room, set down her overnight bag and reached for the wall switch. The floor lamp came on as usual, but it was in the wrong corner. The furniture was the same, but it was out of place, too. "You *changed* it."

He chuckled. "You sound upset."

"Sorry, I didn't mean to. I was just used to it the other way, with the sectional making that U-shape in front of the fireplace."

"I decided to break up the pieces and have a reading nook over in the far corner by the window."

"And that's nice. It just leaves the remaining section in front of the fireplace so... open."

"That's what I was going for. The other arrangement felt too confining."

"I thought it was cozy. The fire's right there and the TV's tucked into that nook on the left. I loved—" Then it hit her. "You did this in May, too, didn't you?"

"I figured you wouldn't have time to come out and watch old movies and TV shows with me anymore." His breath hitched. "I was right."

"Oh, Marsh." She hugged the quilt because hugging him was dangerous. "I should have realized. But I was too self-absorbed to see that I... that you...."

"Don't blame yourself." He set down her suitcase, shoved his hands in the pockets of his jeans and focused on a point over her shoulder. "I thought I was prepared for the day when you told me you were engaged." Meeting her gaze, he didn't try to hide the sadness lurking in his eyes. "Turns out I wasn't. I bought a weight bench, a punching bag, and rearranged my living room. It helped."

His honesty bored a hole in her heart. "Now I'm afraid to ask if we can watch our movies and TV shows while I'm here."

"Of course we can. You didn't marry the guy. And the remaining part of the sectional has plenty of room for both of us."

"You're right. It does." But without the other pieces, the experience would be totally different. Since she was determined to keep their relationship platonic, that was a good thing.

_11_

Having Ella back in his home, something he'd stopped longing for weeks ago, was disconcerting. Lack of sleep didn't help. They could both use some quality time in the sack. Separate quality time.

By a stroke of luck, he'd put on clean sheets early this morning. Or yesterday morning, to be exact. He was a creature of habit, and clean sheets happened on Saturday. Keeping that routine on the day Ella was to be married had made him slightly less crazy.

"Let's get you settled in my room." He picked up her suitcase.

She opened her mouth as if to object.

"Trust me, Ellabella, this is the best arrangement. Just go with it, okay?"

"Okay." She walked down the hall toward his bedroom. "Did you change your room, too?"

"Would you even know if I did?"

"Maybe not. I didn't pay much attention to it when I was over here."

"I didn't change it." No reason to. She'd never spent time there. But now she would sleep in his bed for the next few nights. After she left and he moved back in, he'd have more demons to slay. Couldn't be helped. "Light switch is to the left of the door."

She reached for it and the lamps on either side of the bed came on. "Wow, that's a humungous bed." Walking into the room, she set down the quilt and her overnight bag.

"After sleeping on that twin for years I was ready to stretch out." And now he was picturing stretching out on it with her. He moved a few steps into the room and put down her suitcase. "Well, I'll leave you to—"

"I   remember   that   twin   bed. She turned back to him. "We used to jump on it when your mom was busy in her office."

"Probably didn't improve it, doing that. Anyway, make yourself at—"

"Well, this one's a beauty." Moving closer to the bed, she stroked the varnished peeled log of the nearest post. The honey-colored wood glowed in the lamplight.

Speaking of wood, he was courting disaster the longer he stayed here. "It's all yours. Enjoy." He turned toward the door.

"Don't you want to take some of your stuff out of the bathroom?"

"I can get everything tomorrow." Then his hormone-soaked brain spit out some info. "But now that you mention it, I'll take my toothbrush and toothpaste."

"By all means."

Moving quickly past her, he ducked into the bathroom, switched on the light and glanced around. The porcelain surfaces gleamed. Clean sheet day was also scrub the bathroom day. He couldn't have planned it better.

He picked up his toothbrush and toothpaste. Then he grabbed his razor and shaving cream. Might as well take his deodorant and shampoo while he was at it. And his aftershave. He walked out with his arms full.

She was sitting on the bed, looking like she belonged there. His groin tightened.

She gave him an indulgent smile. "That's better. It's bad enough that you'll be on that fold-out bed. At least you'll be able to shower and shave when you wake up."

"Right." He started out of the room.

"Wait. You need clean undies."

"No, I don't." He kept going.

"Of course you do. Hang on, I'll get you a T-shirt and briefs. Top drawer of the dresser?"

"Never mind. I don't need—"

"Marsh McLintock, I think you're embarrassed."

That pricked his ego. He paused and turned back.

She stood in the doorway, arms crossed. "You brought me a bra today. This is no different."

"Guess not."

"Good. I'll go grab 'em." She disappeared and the drawer squeaked as she opened it. "I assume you want the tighty-whiteys and not the black ones?"

He sighed. "Yes, ma'am." *Play it cool, dude.*

She emerged from the bedroom holding a folded T-shirt and white Jockeys. "I couldn't resist teasing you. Are those sexy black ones for date night?"

"None of your business." And he was blushing. Great.

She laid his underwear on top of his toiletries. "If so, you made a good choice. Unlike my fancy underwire bras, your black briefs are soft and stretchy. You don't have to sacrifice comfort for sex appeal."

"Having fun?"

"Yes. I thought I knew all about you, but I wouldn't have predicted the black briefs."

That stung a little. "Why?"

"Because you're so... sensible."

"And sexually boring?"

"No! I'm sure you're not."

"Are you? Because I get the distinct impression you've categorized me as—"

"Maybe I have." Her voice softened. "Maybe I needed to."

The air left his lungs. "Ella..."

"Good night, Marsh." She turned on her heel and hurried back to his room.

Go after her, idiot! Clint's voice prodded him to take action. Nope. He headed for the spare bedroom. Maybe he was an idiot. Maybe dumping his armload of stuff and following her was the right move and he'd live to regret this decision.

He'd take that chance. After twenty-four years of trusting his instincts when it came to Ella, he wasn't going to stop now. Too much was at stake.

* * *

Marsh's phone jolted him out of a hot dream about Ella. Opening his eyes, he sat up and blinked in the sunlight that hit him in the face, making him squint. What time was it? What was he doing in here?

Oh, yeah. The phone stopped ringing. Silence. At least inside the house. Outside, the birds were making a cheerful racket in the shade trees he'd planted in front to shade the porch. Should've planted one outside *this* window.

The phone pinged with a message. He climbed out of the Murphy bed and stretched. First time he'd slept on it, and he wasn't a fan. Now he was doubly glad he'd insisted Ella take his bed.

She's right down the hall. He felt like he'd swallowed a Slinky. Waking up with Ella in the house sent heat to his privates and cold sweat down his spine.

Until recently she'd been his best buddy, a pal he could count on just like she could count on him. The switch had been flipped when he'd gone with her to the bridal shop and become enamored of her in that dress, but he needed to switch it back.

He picked up his phone from where he'd left it on the weight bench. The room didn't have convenient surfaces to put things he might need over the next week or so. He had a couple of small folding tables that would fix that problem.

The voicemail was from Faye. Hey, Marsh. I left a message for Ella, too. I thought I'd hear from her by now, but she must still be zonked out. Might have turned her phone off, too. Shoot me a text if you hear from her, okay?

He called her back.

"Marsh? I hope I didn't wake you up. I just—"

"You did, but I'm glad you called. She's with me. I mean, not *with* me. She's in my room and I'm in the guest room."

"Ah, so you took her back to your place. That's great. After you guys left, I began to worry that Brit and I should have gone home with you so we could stay with her. She's tough, but under these circumstances, I—"

"I know. I didn't want her to be alone, either." He hesitated. "Last night she sounded like she might want to hang out here for a few days."

"That would be fabulous. She loves it out there. And there's no chance she'll run into you-know-who. I'll bet Mom and Dad will be very happy she's with you instead of alone in her house. I'll pass the word."

"Thanks. She might want some company this week, though. I'll be seeing clients and she'll be working on lesson plans, but if you and Brit—"

"That's a nice idea. I need to prep for my drama classes at UM, but it's not crunch time yet. Tomorrow Brit's back to the nine-to-five routine, but I have some flexibility."

"Good. The weather's great for riding."

"I'd love that."

"So would our foreman Buck. We're all so busy he worries that the horses don't get enough exercise." A subtle whisper of fabric made him turn toward the door.

Ella walked in wearing a white terry robe. "Can I talk to her?"

"Sure." He handed over his phone. As she took it, she gave him a once-over and smiled.

He glanced down. Yep, he'd slept in his Jockeys, answered the phone in his Jockeys and greeted Ella in his Jockeys. Then again, he was in his spare bedroom, not prancing around the house that way.

Scooping up his clothes, including the clean underwear she'd brought him, he made a beeline for the guest bathroom. Thank God he'd taken his other stuff in there before going to bed.

His herky-jerky behavior would likely clue her in to the fact he didn't have much experience with this co-habitating gig. He'd brought his dates out here a few times, but mostly he'd spent the night at their places in town.

So Ella had caught him in his tighty-whities. So what? She hadn't acted as if it bothered her. Maybe he was the only one with a vivid imagination.

Nothing sexy about her robe, thank goodness. Although....

An image flashed through his brain — her smile as she'd looked him up and down, a slight gap in the lapels of her robe as she'd shifted the phone to her other ear, the swell of her cleavage peeking out from under the white terry.

He swallowed. Taking off his briefs, he turned on the cold tap in the shower and stepped under the icy spray.

_12_

"So after Marsh told me about Warner camping out in my living room—"

"That creeps me out, Ella." Faye sounded scared. "Can you report him to the police?"

"On what grounds? He had a key. Anyway, I'll be safe out here." Just _extremely_ frustrated.

"Yeah, that was a good call. I can't picture Warner setting foot on Rowdy Ranch."

"Wanna come out and see me next week?" Faye's presence, even for a few hours, might keep her from doing something stupid.

"Love to! Marsh said the ranch horses need exercise. When?"

The sooner the better. "How about picking up sandwiches and coming out tomorrow around noon? We'll eat here and then drive over to the barn."

"You're on."

"In fact, if you'd also be willing to get some groceries and bring those, I won't feel so much like a mooch. I'll pay you back."

"Just text me a list."

"I will after I take inventory in the morning. Knowing him, he's ready to shoulder the extra expense of having me here, but I'm not about to let him."

"You guys will have a great time. You can geek out on your old movies and TV shows and forget all about Warner. I love this plan."

"It's a good one." Or it had been until five minutes ago, when she'd seen Marsh's considerable attributes cradled in soft white cotton.

When she'd heard him on the phone with Faye, she'd been reaching for the shower knobs. Instead, she'd grabbed a robe and dashed down here, eager to talk to her sister.

She'd pulled up short in the doorway, stunned by the impressive muscle definition in his back, thighs and calves. Clearly he'd hit that workout program hard this summer. Then he'd turned around....

The phone in his hand and her sister on the line had been the only things keeping her from sliding out of her robe and into his arms. Thank God he'd vamoosed.

Recounting the Warner home invasion for her sister had helped her get a grip. Too bad she had excellent hearing and had picked up on the whoosh of the shower.

He was standing under the spray, soaping up that toned body and glorious package. She hadn't allowed herself to speculate on Marsh's endowments. He was more of a Ken doll, or a PC video with the parts below his waist blurred.

Not anymore. Her best friend was hung like a horse.

"Ella?"

"I'm sorry. I got distracted by Marsh's... weight bench. Nice piece of equipment. He works out early in the morning, so that's one reason he insisted I sleep in his bed." She almost choked on that last part. If only he'd insisted on sharing that bed.

But Marsh wasn't like that. He'd listened to her speeches about keeping the friendship free of sexual overtones. He'd do his damnedest to comply. Bless his heart. And his magnificent body. "What were you saying?"

"It wasn't important. I can tell you're still discombobulated. Totally understandable. I'll let you go so you can have a relaxing day with Marsh. He's the perfect person for this situation. He's a healer, after all."

"True." And boy, did she crave some healing.

"Text me your grocery list and I'll be out there around noon tomorrow."

"Excellent. Can't wait."

"Me, either. Oh, and I'll let the folks know your whereabouts, unless you'd rather—"

"I'd appreciate it if you'd tell them. And add in the part about Marsh and me bingeing on our favorite shows, which we plan on doing, by the way. If I know them, their first instinct is to shelter me there, but—"

"Say no more. They're fabulous, but in your shoes, I'd make the same choice."

So would anyone in her shoes, especially if they'd caught a glimpse of Marsh in his skivvies. "Thanks, Faye. See you tomorrow. Love you."

"Love you, too. Give Marsh a hug for me."

"You bet. 'Bye." She'd have to finesse that promise. She didn't dare give him a hug from herself, let alone deliver a proxy hug from Faye.

In order to safely hug Marsh, she'd have to replace the muscular, well-endowed image from this morning with her previous Ken doll version. Could take a while. Like forever.

* * *

While Ella worked with Marsh to fix breakfast, clean up the dishes and unload her stuff from his truck, she faked the palsy-walsy vibe they'd enjoyed for years. Clothes helped. But they didn't make her forget what was covered by his dark blue T-shirt and jeans.

He filled out the shirt way more than he had in May, and she hadn't seen him wear it since then. After she'd become engaged, she'd stopped coming out here. They'd only met for wedding-related reasons and he'd always worn a regular shirt on those days.

At some point he'd bought several new ones and she hadn't made the connection. He'd likely needed a larger size to accommodate his added muscles. She'd been oblivious to his transformation, caught up in her fantasy of a dream wedding and married life with a loving husband and adorable babies.

His biceps flexed as he brought in the last wedding present from the truck, a gift from Desiree. She'd bought a complete set of the dish pattern Ella had chosen. Or to be precise, Ella and

Marsh had chosen. Warner hadn't been interested in making a choice.

He set the box carefully on the floor beside the others in his new reading corner. "She's not going to take these back, you know."

Ella sighed. "But they're so pricey. I wouldn't have even asked for dishes if she hadn't pestered me about it. And she wouldn't have pestered me if you hadn't squealed on me."

"I just told her the truth. You've spent more on Gorilla Glue than you did on those garage sale dishes."

"It's true, and I probably do need to replace them, but I figured she'd get me a couple of place settings to start me off."

He grinned. "Really? Have you met my mother?"

"Good point. She never does anything halfway. Which reminds me. Have you told her I'm here?"

"I texted her while you were getting dressed. She invited us to come over for dinner tonight."

"I'd love that. Just us?"

"I doubt it. Sunday nights tend to be family night, at least for those who can make it."

"Sounds perfect. Did you tell her we'd be there?"

"I will now." Pulling his phone from his back pocket, he tapped quickly and tucked his phone away. "Done." Then he gestured toward the stack of wedding gifts. "Want to tackle this or go for a ride?"

"Gee, I can't decide. Each one is so tempting."

"Then wedding presents it is."

"I was kidding."

"Me, too. I'll call Buck and let him know we'll be taking out Pie and whoever else needs a good run."

"I'll bet you're gonna give me Pie because you feel sorry for me." She adored his chestnut gelding, named after Jimmy Stewart's favorite horse. If her catastrophe of a wedding netted her a ride on Marsh's sweet horse, she'd accept.

"I am giving you Pie, but not because I feel sorry for you, because I don't. You're the luckiest woman alive today. You didn't end up married to Stapleton."

"I am the luckiest woman alive. So why are you giving me Pie?"

"Because you haven't ridden all summer and you're probably rusty." His lips twitched. "Pie is a very tolerant horse."

"Hey. I didn't lose all my skills in three short months. I can handle any horse in that barn."

Laughter simmered in his dark eyes. "Then you don't want Pie?"

"You know I want him. I love riding that horse. I'm just saying—"

"That you don't *need* that horse. You just want him."

"Nicely put." Which begged the question — did she need Marsh or simply want him?

All of the above.

13

Buck asked Marsh to take out Diablo, a flashy black and white Paint who belonged to Rance, his irrepressible younger brother. Rance had asked for extra bartending shifts because he had his eye on a new truck. The longer hours at the Buffalo didn't leave much room for riding, and Diablo was getting more rambunctious by the day.

While Marsh tacked him up, the horse shifted his weight and tossed his head, clearly eager to escape the confines of the barn and the pasture. Marsh talked quietly to him, stroked his neck and promised him a nice long gallop.

"Looks like you have your hands full." Ella had already saddled Pie and mounted up. Not surprising she'd beat him to the punch. That chestnut gelding was the most accommodating horse on the planet.

"We're almost there. He's so excited that he's getting in his own way."

"Good thing you're taking him out, then."

"Yes, ma'am. Probably better that it's me and not Rance. My little brother would likely get into a battle of wills with this animal, which wouldn't do either of them any good."

"How old is Diablo?"

"Young. Just turned seven. Still has a lot of maturing to do."

"He sure is handsome."

"And he knows it. He matches my little brother's personality to a T. Might not be a good thing that they're so much alike. But I can see why Rance picked him."

"I know why you chose Pie."

"Think so?" He checked the cinch one more time and swung into the saddle.

"He matches your personality to a T."

"I suppose he does." She'd meant it as a compliment, so why did it irritate him? Maybe because she was right. Look at how he'd handled this latest crisis — bringing her to his place, giving her his bed and agreeing to stay firmly in the friend zone. Couldn't get more accommodating than that.

"Are we heading out to the meadow?"

"That's the plan. Maybe you should go ahead of me and get the gate. I need to keep a firm hand on this guy."

"Sure thing." She nudged Pie into a trot.

He followed, keeping a tight rein on Diablo. He wanted to blame the horse's dancing hooves on cabin fever, but the gelding could be picking up on his rider's agitated condition.

Had Ella noticed he was on edge? If so, she hadn't commented on it.

His cold shower this morning had been a temporary fix. When she'd waltzed into the kitchen wearing snug jeans and a light blue knit shirt that stretched invitingly over her breasts, he'd been back to square one.

He'd bet she had on one of her comfy bras. And he'd love to confirm that. Only two hooks in the back on those — easily handled.

The jeans cupping her backside tempted him something awful, too. He wanted to peel them off and touch her in a way he never had. Maybe never would.

Funny thing — the outfit wasn't even new. She'd worn those same clothes many times before. But his reaction to it sure was new. How had he spent so much time with this woman and completely overlooked her sexy body?

Evidently he was making up for lost time. Sooner or later she'd catch him ogling, but so far he'd managed to be gazing elsewhere whenever she turned in his direction. Like now, right after she unlatched the gate. Seconds ago he'd been admiring the sweet curve of her ass nestled in the saddle. Close call.

She beckoned him forward. "Go on through. I'll latch it."

"Thanks." Diablo pranced through the opening, neck arched.

"You look impressive on that horse."

"Yes, ma'am. That's what Rance was going for. Had to have the blinged-out saddle, too. He has his heart set on riding Diablo in a parade, but he needs more seasoning."

"Rance or his horse?"

"Both." He turned the Paint in a tight circle to keep him occupied while Ella latched the gate.

Straightening in the saddle, she reached into her boot and pulled out her phone. "Hold him still for a minute. I want a picture."

"I'll do my best, but he's jumpy."

"Maybe I'll do a video, instead, then."

"How about sending it to Rance? A little reminder that he has a horse."

"Good idea." She looped the reins around the saddle horn and pointed the phone in his direction, her tongue stuck in her cheek the way it always was when she took pictures.

The familiar habit made his chest tighten. Her eyes would be narrowed, too, but he couldn't tell because the bill of her cap shaded them.

How she cherished that hat, a faded Wagon Train Cougars cap she'd had since high school. Sometimes she wore it with her hair down, but mostly she pulled it through the opening in the back, like now.

He used to tug on her ponytail when he was teasing her. Hadn't done that in years. How long since he'd touched her hair at all, let alone run his fingers lazily through it, savoring the texture? Only a lover would get to do that.

As the ache in his chest traveled to other parts of his body, he sucked in a breath and glanced toward the meadow a few yards away. "Ready to go?"

"Yep. Just sent the video to Rance." She tucked her phone away and rode toward him. "It's nice out here. I can't believe I went all summer without riding."

"You had a lot to handle." He wheeled Diablo around and pointed him toward the meadow. "I recommend we hold them back a little until the path opens up."

She pulled alongside, bringing the sweet scent of her soap and shampoo with her. "He's acting like a thoroughbred moving toward the starting gate."

"I'm hoping a good run across the meadow will calm him down." With luck, it would have the same effect on his rider.

"Since Diablo's so much younger, will Pie be able to keep up?"

He smiled. "Yes, ma'am. As I recall, I'm usually on Buck's horse when you're riding Pie."

"Right. Dear old Cisco. Is he doing okay?"

"He's great considering his age, but I don't push him. Pie tends to go at the pace the other horse sets, so you've never seen what he's capable of. I advise you to hold on tight."

Her eyes sparkled. "Sounds like fun."

"Ready?"

"So ready."

"On three." He loosened the reins and Diablo quivered in anticipation. "One, two, three, *go.*" He dug in his heels and sent the Paint rocketing across the meadow, his hooves churning up the fragrant earth, his mane flapping in the wind. Grabbing his hat, Marsh hunkered down and laughed as the horse's mane flicked against his cheeks.

"Rock out, Pie!"

He glanced over at Ella, whose grin was as wide as his. True to form, Pie was neck-and-neck with Diablo, his muscles bunching and releasing in perfect time with the Paint's.

Then the scenery blurred. The horse lost significance. There was only Ella, lithe and graceful, riding with the inborn confidence that had made her a star. She was elegance personified, poetry in motion.

He tasted the salty tang of desire on his tongue. He wanted her, had always wanted her. He'd buried the fire deep, lied to himself. Sacrificed his needs on the altar of friendship.

He had no regrets. None. But now she was in his space, closer than ever. Temptation, constantly there, inches away. Could he resist? Maybe. Maybe not.

On the far side of the meadow, he slowly pulled back on the reins. Diablo didn't like that. "Easy, boy, easy."

Ella had an easier time with Pie. "That was awesome! I didn't know Pie could run that fast!"

"Folks underestimate him."

"Clearly I did. I've always loved him because he's such a sweet horse, but *now*... now I know he's got a V-8 under the hood." Leaning down, she hugged him around the neck. "You're even more special than I realized, Pie. You have hidden depths."

So did he, damn it. Great. Now he was jealous of his horse. "Diablo still wants to run. How about a slow canter around the meadow?"

"Sounds good." She cocked her head. "Your boot's ringing."

"So it is." He'd only brought his phone in case of an emergency. His boot muffled the ringtone and he'd been concentrating on Ella. Leaning down, he dragged the phone out, glanced at the screen and tapped it. "Hey, Mom."

"Marsh! I finally got you!"

"What's—"

"Where are you?"

"'In the meadow. We took Pie and—"

"Get over to Beau's. Cut through the woods. It'll be faster. Jess is having the baby and we need—"

"*Having the baby*? Why isn't she in the hosp—"

"No time. The midwife's not answering, for some reason. We need you." She disconnected.

He shoved the phone in his boot and looked at a wide-eyed Ella. "Follow me. We'll take the shortcut."

<u>14</u>

Ella gave Pie his head and the chestnut did a fine job of keeping up with Marsh and Diablo on a faint trail through the forest. Marsh set a fast pace. But that didn't stop him from constantly turning to check on her.

"Just go, Marsh! Don't worry about me. Pie knows the way even if I don't. He'll get me there in one piece."

"He would. But I'm not leaving you."

"Then trust that I'm right behind you and stop looking over your shoulder. I promise to call out if I'm falling behind."

"Okay."

They made better progress after that. Glimpses of the back porch of Beau and Jess's log cabin appeared through the trees. The area beside it looked like a used car lot. Some vehicles Ella recognized — Beau's dark red truck, Sky's silver one, and Desiree's royal purple F-350. Jess's forest-green SUV was the only passenger car in the mix.

Snatches of conversation drifted from the front of the house. The McLintocks had gathered.

Marsh skirted the pen where Beau kept Slim and Pickens, his pot-bellied pigs. Ella glanced over as she rode past. Wow, they'd grown. They stood by the fence, snouts pressed against the fence while they made little grunting sounds.

"Ella, you'd better stay with the horses while I go inside." He rode over to the back porch and quickly dismounted.

"Be glad to." She came up beside him and swung down from the saddle.

"Pie's good with a ground-tie, but—"

"Just get in there." He was clearly flustered if he felt the need to explain something she knew as well as he did. "I'll handle these guys." She ducked under Pie's neck and took hold of Diablo's bridle.

"I don't know how long—" A cry of pain from inside the house grabbed his attention.

"Go."

He hurried toward the steps and took them two at a time. The sounds of distress grew louder as he opened the back door and slipped inside.

Maintaining her hold on a restless Diablo, she unwound the reins from Pie's saddle horn and dropped them to the ground. Although the chestnut's ears pricked forward, he stayed where he was.

"Good boy, Pie. Good boy." Ella gave him a pat and focused on Diablo. He'd started dancing whenever a fresh set of cries laced with swear words issued from the house. "Come on, big guy. Let's go see those pigs." She led him away from the porch and guided him toward the pigpen.

The noise from the cabin faded a little. Not completely, though. That would require noise canceling headphones for her and the Paint. The image made her smile.

When Slim, the all-black piggy, spotted her approaching with Diablo, he trotted back to the fence with short barks of welcome. His little brother Pickens followed, his tail wagging so hard his whole backend wiggled.

"Hey, guys, you sure have gotten big. Bet the two of you can't fit in the passenger seat of Beau's truck anymore."

They gazed up at her and grinned. She'd dare anyone to see that expression and call it something else.

"You're cute as ever, though. I brought you a friend." She turned to the Paint, who'd lowered his head to get a better look. "You and Pickens have the same black-and-white style going on, Diablo. Pickens is built a bit lower to the ground, but otherwise, you could be twins."

Diablo snorted and the pigs let out barks of alarm as they backed up a few feet.

"It's okay, piggies. He means you no harm." She crouched down. "Wish I had some treats for you guys, but I didn't know I'd be seeing you today."

The woof, woof sound from the pigs increased in volume as they hurried toward her and shoved their noses against the fence again.

"Whoops. I forgot you speak English. I shouldn't have said the T word." Diablo's breath tickled her ear. "Don't look now, guys, but Diablo's acting like he wants to make friends." She edged away, giving Diablo space to touch noses with the pigs.

She held very still as horse and piggies made brief contact through the wire fence. Then Diablo snorted again, sending the pigs scurrying backward with barks of protest.

"Oh, well. Friendships take time. We'll label this a work in progress." She stood and looped her arm around Diablo's neck. "They're younger than you, buddy, just kids. Let's give them a break."

No response from Diablo.

"With a little effort, you could gain their trust. My money's on you. As the mature one of the group, you need to lead by example." She'd given the same speech to a troubled teenager last semester. Maybe it was fanciful to give it to Diablo, but it couldn't hurt.

"Ella?"

She glanced toward the porch and rose to her feet.

Beau, looking pale and shaken, gripped the railing as if needing the support. "Why are you out here by yourself?"

"We came in the back way and Marsh left me in charge of the horses." She maintained a steady grip on Diablo's bridle as she peered at Beau. "Are you okay?"

"No, ma'am." He flinched as more yelling and cursing spilled from the cabin. "The doc warned us she'd be a sizeable baby. My fault."

"Beau, you can't blame—"

"Jess was supposed to get drugs, but Maverick came so fast we didn't..." His voice shook and he waved a hand toward the door. "Now Jess..." He bowed his head. "She has to gut it out."

She would have climbed the steps and hugged him if she dared leave Diablo. Not possible. "Beau, this is not your fault."

He lifted his head, his eyes filled with misery. "Feels like it is."

"Well, it's not."

He took a shaky breath. "Marsh told me to take a break. He could tell I was about to pass out or start bawling."

"But she's okay, right?"

"Marsh says her vital signs are good. Mom's in there, and Marybeth. And Jess's dad. They're all saying positive stuff. It's just… I know it hurts like hell. Wish I could do it for her." He shuddered as Jess let out another string of swear words.

"It's better that she's yelling, though. Coach used to tell us that suffering in silence is bad for you, physically and mentally."

He nodded. "That helps. Thanks." Sucking in another breath, he started down the steps. "I'll take you and the horses around front. There's a passel of folks out there who could babysit that spoiled animal. I'll bet Rance is one of them."

"All right." She agreed as much for Beau's sake as hers. He clearly needed to walk off some of that guilt and anxiety before he went back in.

When he took charge of Diablo, she scooped up Pie's reins and followed him around the parked vehicles to the front yard. The McLintock clan stood in small clusters, with no one availing themselves of the rockers on the porch. Looked like they wanted to stay close to the action, but not too close.

As usual, the men outnumbered the women, but not the way they used to in this family. Now Sky's wife Penny and Cheyenne's fiancée Kendall helped even the odds.

Sky broke away from a group that included Penny and Buck. As his brisk strides carried him toward Beau and Diablo, he raised his voice. "Come get your horse, Rance."

"I'm coming, I'm coming." Rance jogged over. "I got your video, Ella. Did you and Marsh just get here? Is he—"

"He's—" Beau cleared his throat. "Marsh is inside with Jess."

Sky put a hand on Beau's shoulder, eyebrows lifted in a silent question.

"Everything's fine. Marsh has it under control. He suggested I... needed fresh air."

"I get that."

"Anyway, I walked out on the back porch and found Ella and Diablo talking to the pigs." A wail from the cabin sent his attention skittering in that direction. "Somebody please take Diablo. I gotta go."

"I've got him." Rance gripped the Paint's bridle as Beau turned the horse over to his little brother and took off, lengthening his strides on the way to the porch.

"Who's seen Beau?" Desiree's voice was unnaturally shrill as she shoved open the front door. "Oh, there you are. She's calling for you."

"I hear her." He pounded up the steps.

"Give her our love, Beau," Angie called out.

"I will, sis!" He followed his mother into the house and closed the door, slightly muting the drama going on inside.

"I'll take Pie, too." Rance held out his hand for Pie's reins. "Thanks for minding these two, Ella."

"You're welcome." She hesitated. "What are you going to do with them? You can't just stick them in the pen with the pigs."

"I'll walk 'em around, maybe meander down the road and back. Settle 'em down a little."

She prickled at that. She'd done a good job calming Diablo by taking him to visit Slim and Pickens. "Actually, they're both—"

"You do that, Rance," Sky said. "Good idea."

Ella handed over the reins and Rance led the horses down a graded dirt road.

Sky lowered his voice. "He didn't mean to insult your wrangler skills. He's freaking out."

"Am not," Rance called over his shoulder. "Just thinking of these animals."

Ella waited until he was out of earshot. "Rance isn't the only one freaking out."

"I noticed." Sky nudged back his hat and gazed toward the house. "Never seen Beau this rattled."

"He hates that she's suffering."

"Can't say I'd be doing any better if it was Penny. I can't imagine encouraging the woman I love to go through something like this."

"Are you having second thoughts about kids?"

He turned back to her. "Second, third and fourth thoughts. But Penny's a warrior. I just asked her a few minutes before you showed up if she wanted to reconsider. Nope. She'll put up with whatever." He shook his head. "I had no idea it could be like this."

"Really? You and your siblings must have been hefty babies. Surely your mom must have mentioned—"

"My mother is a miracle of nature. She loved being pregnant and she describes giving birth as *slightly uncomfortable.*"

"That's remarkable."

"She's one in a million." Jess's next bellow of pain made him suck in a breath. "And because of that, Beau wasn't prepared for—"

"*Halleluuuuujaaaah!*" Jess's voice rang out like a Chinese gong. "I diiiiid it! She's heeeeere!"

A new sound came from the cabin, a rhythmic, scratchy newborn cry as Maverick McLintock announced her arrival.

Relieved laughter and cheers erupted. The newly minted aunts and uncles milled around like bumper cars, hugging and high-fiving each other. Ella joined in, congratulating everyone. Some were so punch-drunk with joy they congratulated *her.* Maybe she'd end up an honorary aunt. That would be more than okay

She'd just paused long enough to ask Cheyenne and Kendall about their wedding plans when the front door burst open and Marybeth rushed out, cheeks rosy, her signature gray braid coming undone. "She's beautiful!"

"When can we see her, Marybeth?" Cheyenne shouted back.

"Soon, real soon!" She spun around to head inside and collided with Jess's dad as he barreled through the doorway.

He turned the collision into an enthusiastic hug before he ushered her inside. Then he faced the crowd with a smile so big his eyes almost disappeared. "I got to *hold* her. She's *amazing.*"

"Hey, Andy," Clint said. "How soon will they bring her—"

"Soon as they clean her up. Who wants a cigar?" He nearly tripped coming down the steps. "I have real ones and bubblegum ones." He pulled them out of a fanny pack and circulated through the gathering.

Kendall grinned. "I should blow his mind and take a real cigar."

"I should, too."

Kendall shook her head. "You won't get away with it, Ella. You're a star athlete. I'm an unknown quantity. I could light up that sucker right in front of him and he wouldn't question it."

"I dare you."

"Don't say that, Ella." Cheyenne glanced at his petite fiancée. "She can't resist a dare."

"But I will this time, sugar lips."

Sugar lips? Was the muscular firefighter putting up with that? Ella ducked her head to hide a grin.

Cheyenne didn't even blink. "Why?"

"I tried one of my dad's cigars when I was ten and nearly choked to death. But you go ahead."

"Not my thing."

"And here he comes." Kendall raised her voice. "We'll each take bubblegum, please, Mr. Hartmann."

"Okey-dokey. And call me Andy." He dug three out of his fanny pack. "At this rate I may run out of the bubblegum ones. More gum-chewers than smokers in this crowd."

"Mom's not a fan of cigar smoke," Cheyenne said.

Andy nodded. "I didn't know that. Thanks, son. Good information."

"But you must like them," Ella said.

"Used to love a good cigar, especially after I put the *Sentinel* to bed. But I hardly ever smoke 'em anymore. Just wanted to carry on the tradition. I passed out cigars when Jess was born."

Ella put her pink bubblegum cigar in her pocket. "Mom says my dad did the same when my sister and I were born. Speaking of that, I should call Faye. She'll want to hear the news."

"You should because it won't be in the *Sentinel* for another week."

Ella smiled. "Not going to put out a special edition?"

"My accountant would kill me, but look for a fancy poster in the window tomorrow." He tipped his Stetson and moved on.

"'Scuse me, guys." Ella glanced at Cheyenne and Kendall. "I need to call Faye."

"No worries," Kendall said. "I should check with Angie about our schedule tomorrow, see if this changes anything."

"That's right, you two are doing the handywoman gig together, now. How's it going?"

"Great. We're having fun and making money at the same time."

"Excellent! Oh, by the way, I just remembered I want to ask Angie something."

"Want me to ask her?"

"Sure. I'd like to borrow her boxing gloves so I can try out Marsh's punching bag."

"I'll let her know."

"Thanks." After Kendall and Cheyenne walked away, she pulled her phone from her boot and called Faye, who was excited for Beau and Jess and wanted pictures if Ella could get some shots of Maverick.

Ella promised to do her best. Then she disconnected and paused, taking time to absorb the happy sounds of people celebrating. Was this scene what she'd envisioned when she'd accepted Warner's proposal?

Yep. Her parents and Faye would be looking and acting like Andy, beside themselves with joy. Now that Warner was out of the picture, some generic guy stood by her side as she cradled their precious child. And Marsh would be there, of course, surveying the happy family with fondness and love.

Or not. Maybe he'd be out on his back porch, his fists crashing into his punching bag. He might have bought the bag and the weight bench because she'd made a bad choice. But what if he would have been upset no matter who she'd chosen?

If she asked him point-blank, he'd tell her the truth. Did she want to know? His answer could complicate an already tricky situation.

"Listen up, folks." Buck used his foreman-of-the-ranch voice to get everyone's attention. "Marybeth just texted me. They're coming out, and we need to be quiet and peaceful-like so we don't scare little Maverick."

"Got it," Sky said.

"Since she's so brand-new," Buck continued, "they'll stay up on the porch and they've asked us to stay down here. Beau will hold her up so we can all get a good look at the little tyke."

Clint chuckled. "Anybody else thinking *Lion King*?"

"Me," Rance said. "And I've got that tune on my phone. I could—"

"Stifle that urge." Sky gave him a look. "We don't need you blasting *The Circle of Life* from your phone."

"I could play it softly. It would be so funny."

Ella agreed with Rance, but Buck and Sky might not be in the mood for hilarity.

"It would," Clint said. "C'mon, Sky. It's a cute idea."

Sky glanced over at Buck. "You okay with that?"

"Let me text Marybeth."

"Don't tell her the song," Rance said. "Just say it'll be some soft music."

"All right." He concentrated on his phone. "Marybeth says it's okay if it's not loud. They'll be out in about two minutes. Keep it low, son." He tucked his phone away.

"I will, I promise."

"If you'll be fooling with your phone, I'd better take Diablo and Pie off your hands." Buck walked over and gripped both bridles. "Now you can move up front for your ten seconds of fame."

"Thanks." Rance took his position by the bottom step and scrolled through his phone. Then he turned back to the group. "You know what would be even funnier? If you'd all kneel down like the animals did in the movie."

"Nope." Sky shook his head. "Not doing that."

"Me neither," Clint said. "Not my style. But we could take off our hats."

Cheyenne glanced at his twin. "I like that idea, Clint. Let's do it." He surveyed the group. "Hats off, guys?"

Sky nodded. "That works."

"We'll be taking our hats off, too, big brother." Angie glanced at Penny, Kendall and Ella. "Right ladies?"

"Absolutely," Penny said.

"And here they come." Sky moved closer to his wife and put his arm around her waist.

Ella positioned herself near Rance, eager to get pictures for Faye. And to see Marsh, the hero of the hour. Again. His knowledge and calming presence had brought the first McLintock grandchild safely into the world. Heady stuff.

Marybeth and Desiree came out first, looking as if they'd been ridden hard and put away wet. Their shirts were untucked and their hair stuck out every which way, but their radiant expressions eclipsed their raggedy appearance. Emotion tightened Ella's throat.

Beau came next, moving slowly as he helped Jess out the door, a blanket-wrapped bundle in her arms. Marsh was right behind her and moved into place so he could support her from the other side.

A collective sigh traveled through the crowd gathered at the foot of the stairs. Ella's breath whooshed out, too, but her reaction was tied to the man looking straight at her. He was as mussed as everyone else on the porch, his sleeves rolled to his elbows, his shirttail hanging out, his hair damp with sweat. Sexy.

But it was his gaze, which immediately locked with hers, that made her dizzy. She'd faced players on the court wearing that expression. A player with that level of intensity had a goal and the drive to achieve it.

Anticipation tingled in her veins.

15

Marsh couldn't wait to be alone with Ella. Couldn't happen now, though. Probably just as well. He knew what he wanted but hadn't figured out the best way to get it.

The drama of delivering Beau and Jess's baby had shaken him to the core. After it was over and he'd caught his breath, he'd taken stock. Lo and behold, his attitude and his priorities had changed.

Not surprising, considering the intensity in that birthing room. In the final moments, his mom and Jess's dad had each gripped one of Jess's hands. Both grandparents had the bruises to prove how hard she'd squeezed.

Marybeth had run around with a towel mopping sweaty faces and cheerleading like crazy.

He and Beau had knelt together at the foot of the bed as Jess had gritted her teeth and pushed with every muscle in her body.

Her fierce determination had finally paid off. At long last, Maverick had slid into Marsh and Beau's outstretched hands and everyone in the room had sobbed with relief. Everyone.

He'd walked out of that room a different man. He was no longer willing to accept the status quo. But he needed Ella's cooperation to change it.

Before he talked with her, he'd settle on the best approach. Maybe he'd — wait, music was coming from somewhere. It would be just like Beau to use his phone to jazz up the occasion.

Except it wasn't Beau. Rance stood at the foot of the steps, his arm stretched skyward. As Beau unwrapped the blanket covering Maverick and held her up, *The Circle of Life* poured from Rance's phone.

Marsh's grin turned into a chuckle, then a mostly silent belly laugh.

Jess snorted. "I can't believe he did that."

"Well, I love it." Beau lifted Maverick higher and began to sing along.

First their mom joined in, followed by Marybeth. When Jess started singing, Marsh did, too.

The chuckles and smothered laughter from the family members morphed into a chorus of voices crooning the lyrics. Ella swayed in place as she sang, her eyes shining with delight.

And there it was, the element he was missing. Playfulness. He'd go with that. *Thanks, Rance.*

Then Sky took off his hat and laid it over his heart. Everyone followed suit. As the music swelled to a climactic finish, the singing took on a richer tone as the McLintocks celebrated the arrival of new life — the beginning of the next generation.

Marsh's raw emotions took another hit. His eyes filled with tears. He blinked them away, took a deep breath and squared his shoulders. Breaking down in the birthing room was one thing. Doing it in front of his entire family... not happening.

He snuck a peek at Beau. His brother had returned Maverick to Jess's arms and bowed his head. Great idea. Marsh studied his boots until he had regained control. Then, as the song ended, he looked up.

After an audible sniff, Beau did, too. "Thank you." He soldiered on, his voice hoarse. "I love this family, but I've never loved you more than right now." He paused to swallow. "When Maverick's old enough, I'll tell her how you honored her today."

"It was Rance's idea," Sky said.

"Clint gave it to me, though." Rance looked uncharacteristically shy about claiming the spotlight. "And taking off our hats was Sky's idea."

Jess cleared her throat. "That was the part that got me. Like you were taking her into your hearts."

"Which we were." Sky's voice was husky, too. "But hey, you and Beau must be exhausted. Thank you for bringing her out, but you don't have to stay. Go get some rest."

"I believe we will." She glanced up at Beau. "Ready for a nap?"

"Yes, ma'am." He turned to the crowd. "We'll surface in a few days. Oh, and the party's at Mom's." He gave her a wink. "I'm assuming."

"You assume right. Head over to Rowdy Roost, everybody. We'll throw something together."

Marsh turned to Jess. "I'll help you get settled before I leave, though."

Marybeth and his mom converged on them. "We will, too."

"Put me to work." Andy hopped up on the porch. "I'm here to serve."

Beau swept a glance over each of them. "I owe you all more than I can ever repay. Now it's time for you to go have fun. We've got this."

"We absolutely do," Jess said. "We'll be fine. If we have an issue, we'll call. Otherwise, we'll see you... soon."

Marybeth smiled. "I think we're being dismissed."

"No!" Jess looked horrified. "We would never—"

"I'm teasing, sweetheart. You need time alone. Just remember we're only a phone call and less than ten minutes away."

"That's comforting," Beau said. "And it's why I'm okay with sending you guys home. Trust me, you'll hear from us if we screw up."

"You won't." Marybeth patted his arm.

Marsh glanced toward the yard, which was rapidly emptying. Ella stood talking with Rance and Buck was nearby minding the horses. "I rode over here on Diablo. With Ella and Pie."

"Just because you rode over doesn't mean you have to ride back. Buck and Rance can take care of getting the horses home. You and Ella can ride in the truck with me. I'll fetch your hat from the house." Marybeth motioned him toward the steps. "Go on down. Tell them the plan."

"Yes, ma'am." Loosening his hold on Jess, he turned to face the tired but happy new parents. "Call me if *anything* comes up. I mean it."

Jess smiled. "I know you do because you're terrific. I want you to deliver all our babies."

"You're only saying that because you're high on endorphins. But thanks." He gave her shoulder a squeeze, gently stroked Maverick's tiny cheek, and hugged Beau tight. His brother responded with a one-armed hug that nearly busted one of Marsh's ribs.

Marybeth showed up with his hat and smiled. "Can't bear to leave 'em, can you?"

"I'm going. Thanks for the hat." He tipped it in the direction of the new family and followed Marybeth down the steps.

As she approached Buck, she gestured in Marsh's direction. "This poor man's been through it today. If you and Rance will ride these horses back to the barn, I'll take Marsh and Ella to the party in our truck."

"Much as I appreciate that offer," Marsh said, "I'd like to ride back on Diablo, after all. It would give me time to decompress. I can't speak for Ella, though."

She glanced at him and nodded. "I'd like that, too. It's a pretty trail through the pines. I didn't see much of it on the way over."

"That'll make my life easier," Rance said. "If I leave my truck here and ride Diablo, then I'll have to—" He caught himself. "But I'll totally ride him back if you need me to, Marsh. Heck, I'll ride him and lead Pie so Buck doesn't have to do it. No problem at all. Seriously."

"Relax, little brother." Marsh thumbed back his hat. "Take your truck. I'll ride Diablo back."

"You're sure? Did he give you trouble? He probably did, didn't he? I know I need to—"

"He was fine. And playing *The Circle of Life* was inspired. Good call."

Rance flushed. "Thanks, Marsh." He hesitated. "What was it like in there? It sounded bad."

What was it like? Life-changing. "Jess had a rougher time than she'd planned on, but she made it through and now she and Beau have a daughter. Jess would probably say it was worth it."

"Made me glad I'm a guy."

"Me, too. Now get out of here, bro. I'm sure Mom could use some help with the party."

"Right. She'll need me behind the bar. See you all there." He tipped his hat and left, his back straight and his stride purposeful.

Buck gazed after him. "I think maybe that boy's growing up."

"I agree." Marybeth watched him climb into his truck. "Seeing his devil-may-care role model become a father must be sobering."

"I reckon it had that effect on all the boys." Buck laid a hand on Marsh's shoulder. "It eased my mind, knowing you were in there, son."

"Thank you, sir." Marsh's chest warmed with pleasure. Buck wasn't the type to scatter praise like chicken feed.

His weathered face creased in a smile when he turned to Ella. "I understand you're partial to Marsh's horse."

"I love him."

"That makes you a good judge of horseflesh, Miss Ella." Buck handed over the reins. "There's not a finer horse in the barn. I'm partial to this chestnut, myself."

She swung into the saddle, graceful as always. "I'll take good care of him."

"I have no doubt."

Marsh mounted Diablo, who stood quietly instead of dancing around. "Hey, Buck, did you give this horse a talking to?"

"Wasn't necessary. He's had some exercise, a change of scenery and the influence of an older, wiser horse. He knows you won't put up with his nonsense. This is good training for him, you on Diablo and Ella on Pie."

"Maybe we'll have time for another ride or two this week." He glanced at Ella.

"Fine with me."

He tipped his hat to Buck and Marybeth. "See you back at the house." He nudged Diablo into a trot and Ella kept pace with him.

As they rode through the backyard, Beau's laughter filtered out through an open window.

Marsh exchanged a smile with Ella. "Good to hear."

"Sure is." She glanced over at Slim and Pickens, their noses pressed against the fence again. "Is there any chance he'll forget to feed those guys?"

"I seriously doubt it, especially if he leaves the window open. They can make a racket when they want to."

"Then I won't worry about it. Or Beau and Jess. They've been through a trial by fire. You, too, I'm guessing."

"Yes, ma'am." He'd bonded with his older brother in a way neither would have chosen, in a flood of tears. But even though he cherished their new closeness, he'd rather not repeat that routine.

He looked over at her as they approached the narrow path into the woods. "Okay if I lead?"

"Sure. Diablo probably likes that better. And Pie just goes with the flow."

"Yes, he does." His rider usually did the same. Not today.

The air cooled as he left the sunny clearing for the tree-shaded riding trail. He breathed in pine-scented air as Diablo crushed fallen needles under his hooves.

Was there a meadow along this trail? He hadn't ridden it enough to say for sure. He'd look for one. Nudging Diablo into a faster trot, he kept his eyes peeled.

"Must have been a tense situation in the cabin."

"It was tense. And thought-provoking."

"You had time to think? While Jess was yelling like crazy?"

"Not during the process. After the process. You know what they say about witnessing a birth."

"Actually, I don't. What do they say?"

Damned if he knew. He was making this up as he went along. "Birth is one of the profound mysteries of life." Hey that wasn't half bad.

"I suppose it is. I've never witnessed a human birth, but I've been there for kittens and puppies. That's always amazing. Delivering Beau and Jess's child must have been awe-inspiring."

"Sure was. And experiencing a profound mystery leads you to think of other mysteries." Like why he'd never kissed Ella. He'd had twenty-five years to accomplish it.

"I thought you wanted to talk about the actual event so you could decompress."

"That was easier to say than admitting I wanted to contemplate life's mysteries. I'd sound like a fruitcake."

"What sort of mysteries?"

"Oh, several." Like whether there was a meadow up ahead.

"Alrighty, then. Go for it."

"It'll be better if we're face-to-face."

"You're gonna ride backward?"

"Too complicated. I'll just turn Diablo around and put him in reverse."

She laughed. "If you were on Pie, I'd believe you."

He made her laugh. So far, so good. "If there's a meadow on this trail, we could stop for a bit."

"Okay."

Her lilting tone told him she was getting curious about this detour. Not a bad starting point.

"Can you give me a hint about this mystery?"

"It has to do with our friendship."

"What about it?"

"I'll tell you when we're looking at each other. And sure enough, we've found us a meadow."

"Good thing we did. I can't wait to find out what this friendship mystery is."

"I can't wait to tell you." He was pumped, and not as nervous as he'd been when they'd started out. She was in the right mood. This could work.

Guiding Diablo into the meadow, he jumped down and dropped the reins to the ground. "Diablo, *stay.*"

"He's not a dog, Marsh."

"No harm in trying. It could work." Walking away as if he trusted the gelding to do as he was told, he helped Ella down and ground-tied Pie.

She gazed at him. "Okay, we're face-to-face. What's the mystery?"

First he checked on Diablo, who stood quietly, obeying orders. Then he took off his hat and hung it on Pie's saddle horn. "I was thinking about all the adventures we've had together, all the fun times."

She smiled. "Yes, we have. I treasure them all, even jumping off the roof."

"I treasure them, too, except for the pie-eating contest."

"Don't get me started."

"I won't. I don't want to talk about the pie-eating contest, especially in front of my horse."

"Oh, my God! How did I not realize that you ended up with a horse named Pie?" She grinned. "I can't believe I never made the connection."

"Trust me, it wasn't on purpose. Just a strange coinkidink." He rested his hands on her shoulders and resisted the urge to pull her close.

Sunlight pierced the canopy of pines, just enough to bring out the amused sparkle in her blue eyes and the soft pink of her smiling lips.

He took a deep breath. Crunch time. "It's come to my attention that we're missing a golden opportunity to have an adventure doing something we've never tried before. It's a mystery why we haven't. We're both in shape for it."

"I can't imagine what you're talking about. What adventure?"

"I'm talking about sex, Ellabella. Sex between good friends."

16

Ella gulped as her insides turned into a pinball machine and she got the shakes. ""Marsh, that's not an adventure. That's a disaster in the making."

He pressed a hand to his chest. "You wound me, madam. I have it on good authority that I'm a fairly decent partner."

Darn him, now she was tingling. "That's not the point! Sex would wreck everything."

"Why assume that? Why couldn't we dive into it like any other physical activity and come out smiling?"

"Because it's not like any other physical activity and you know it."

"Okay, I'll agree with you that we've never tried a sport where we're naked, but that's part of the adventure, part of the challenge."

"You're insane." She couldn't stop quivering. Was it from stress or excitement? Couldn't tell the difference. Especially when he stood so close she could see the little gold flecks in his brown eyes. And the tempting shape of his mouth.

"Hear me out. It's made to order for our current situation. We're temporarily living together. Nobody has to know what we're up to."

A secret liaison. Her breath hitched. "You think they wouldn't guess?"

"Not if we play it cool when we're with the family. I know you have a game face. Use it."

The clandestine nature of his suggestion appealed to her. He knew which buttons to push. But she would resist. Had to, for both their sakes. "There's no good reason to take such a reckless chance with our friendship."

"I can think of two." He held up one finger. "I want you." He put up a second finger. "And you want me."

"You're making a big assumption on that second part, buster."

"Am not. I know you better than almost anyone does. You want me bad."

He was right. She began to panic. "Look, Marsh. We've kept that promise we made to each other for—"

"Time to break it."

"Just like that?" She stepped back, dislodging his grip. "After twenty years?"

"You just made my point. The timing is perfect. If we'd tried this when we were younger, we wouldn't have had the maturity to handle it. We'd let messy emotions get in the way."

"Are you saying you could have sex with me just for the fun of it?"

"Yes. I'll have more fun sex with you than I've ever had with anyone because I know you so well. We've been preparing for this adventure for years."

As her resistance ebbed, she took another step back. "Stop talking like this. We're best friends. *Best friends*! I'm not endangering that special relationship for some silly old sex."

He smiled. "Now you're getting the idea. We'll have silly sex, but it won't be old. It'll be totally new, something we've never experienced together."

"What we have is a bone-deep loyalty that will last forever." She glared at him. "Unless you ruin it."

"*We* won't ruin it. We'll enhance it, add a new level of understanding. Let me be clear. I'm not suggesting we have a romantic relationship. We'll be exploring our sexual selves within the safe confines of a deep and abiding friendship. What could be better?"

"Maintaining our current celibate status."

"Think you can do that? Living in my house? Sleeping in my bed?"

She glanced away. He was on the money, making logical points she couldn't refute. "If I want you so much, why haven't I seduced you before now?"

"Because you're chicken."

"What?"

"You heard me. You like to think you're the more adventurous one, but when it comes to the most exciting adventure of all, you're scared stiff."

"Are you seriously putting sex in the same category as jumping off the roof?"

"Why not? It's a whole lot safer. We won't have to worry about breaking a leg."

She peered at him. "This is a joke, isn't it?" *Please let it be a joke.*

"I'm not joking, but we'll definitely have some laughs along the way."

Why did he have to stand there looking at her like that, daring her to find out exactly what he had under those Jockeys? "It's a very bad idea."

"I'm surprised you'd say that. Aren't you the one who had to distance yourself from me at the reception last night because you found me irresistible?"

"I'd just discovered my fiancé was a lying, cheating bastard. And there you were, being wonderful. It's only natural that I—"

"Discovered your best friend is hot?"

"No. I mean, yes, I'll admit you turn me on a little." She crossed her arms. "But I cherish you as the best friend any person could ever have. I have some pesky thoughts, especially after seeing your, um, attributes on display this morning. Don't you own any pajamas?"

He had the nerve to flash her a sexy smile. "Normally I sleep naked. Leaving the Jockeys on was in deference to having you in the house."

"Naked? No!" A jolt of awareness targeted her lady parts. "You're supposed to have a pair of those plaid PJs with an elastic waist bottom and button-up top."

His smile became a teasing grin. "It that's what turns you on, I'll buy some tomorrow."

"This *is* a joke. It has to be. If I just wait you out, eventually you'll crack up and tell me never mind, you were only kidding."

"Don't count on it." He moved closer. "You don't have to decide now. We're due at Mom's party. But once we get back to my place, I'll need to know your answer."

"I'll give it to you right now. The answer is no."

He laughed and made clucking noises.

"Stop that."

"How can you give me your answer now? You don't have enough information to make an informed decision."

"I have all the information I need."

He came within touching distance. Heat flickered in his eyes. "You have no idea what you're rejecting. We've never kissed."

"Yes, we have."

"That doesn't qualify."

Her insides quivered. "A kiss is just a kiss."

"That's where you're wrong, Ellabella." He slid his arms around her waist and took off her hat, sending her hair tumbling to her shoulders.

She should stop him. Except those velvet lips had made an impression yesterday when she'd been the one initiating the action. What would they feel like when the kiss was his idea? "Oh, for heaven's sake. Go ahead and kiss me. It won't change anything."

"We'll see about that." He drew her close, making contact right down the line — chest, hips, thighs.

She gasped. Dozens of friendly hugs and hours on the dance floor hadn't prepared her for an embrace clearly meant to arouse. She warmed at every significant juncture and battled the urge to snuggle even closer.

If she responded like this when they were wearing clothes, what would happen when... no, not *when. If.* She'd agreed to nothing beyond this kiss. She could handle one little kiss.

But when his lips touched down, there was nothing little about it. He took full possession of her mouth, both outside and in. He didn't coax, he commanded. The guy she'd labeled a perfect gentleman... wasn't.

The moves he made with his tongue left no doubt as to his plans if she agreed to this crazy scheme. Her core clenched in response. When her legs turned to rubber and her panties grew damp, she clutched his shoulders for support. Who was this guy? She'd had no clue.

He pressed his aroused body closer. God help her, she pushed back. And moaned.

Tightening his grip, he slowly lifted his mouth, his breathing as ragged as hers. "Are we having fun, yet?"

Squeezing her eyes shut, she fought through the waves of lust to create a complete sentence. "You caught me off-guard. Next time I'll be ready for—"

"So there'll be a next time?" His breath was warm on her wet, tingling lips

"I didn't say that."

"I think you did."

"Please let me go, Marsh." He released her, and when she wobbled, he gripped her forearms to steady her, but he didn't try to pull her back into his arms. She looked up and got lost in the warm glow of his gaze. "I need time to think."

"That's better than the solid no you gave me before."

"I need my hat back."

"Yes, ma'am." He handed it to her.

"You're good at this kissing business." Pulling her hair through the back of the cap helped settle her down.

"So are you."

"I didn't do anything."

"You gave me a warm welcome."

She had nothing to say to that. Once again, he was right. "I still think it's a bad idea. Having sex will change us."

"Isn't that what new experiences are all about?"

"You keep making it sound like we're enrolling in a kickboxing class."

"I would argue that it's very much like that. Substitute aerobic sexual activity for kickboxing and—"

"Sex is not a competitive sport."

"Then how about yoga? No, wait — combine yoga and country swing and you have all the elements — creative body movement in cooperation with a partner."

"Delivering Jess and Beau's baby inspired you to come up with this plan? Because I question that. I don't see how—"

"It wasn't so much the event as the realization that when we're born, we're given a certain number of days on Earth. Once we're of age, it's up to us how we use those days."

"And you want to use the next few days having fun sex with me?"

"Fun, friendly sex. Yes, ma'am, I do."

"I'll think about it during the party, but it's only fair to warn you that despite that spectacular kiss, I—"

"Spectacular?" He beamed at her. "I was pretty sure you liked it, but I appreciate the five-star spectacular review."

"You deserve it. That said, when I listen to my inner voice, it tells me to say no."

"Funny, but my inner voice is telling me to go for it."

"Then I guess we'll see which inner voice wins out. Oh, and in case you're hoping that a few beers or bottles of cider will mellow me out, think again. I'll be sipping non-alcoholic beverages tonight."

"Glad to hear it. The first time I take you to bed, I want you to be on your game. I'm looking for the woman who dominated the boards during the state championship."

She studied him. "Can you swear to me that you just came up with this idea today?"

"Yes, ma'am, I can. Why?"

"Because when you throw in a reference to the game I played when I was eighteen, it makes me wonder... have you been hoping for this outcome since we were in high school?"

He hesitated. "I didn't think so."

"Hmm."

"Look, Ella, this isn't a life plan. It's just sex."

She gazed at him. "Have you ever had *just sex*?" She added air quotes to emphasize her point.

"Well..."

"Didn't think so." Taking his hat off Pie's saddle, she handed it to him. "Let's go to the party. Before we leave, I'll give you my decision." And pray she had enough self-control to make the right one.

17

Marsh usually had a blast at family parties, and if he didn't want to arouse suspicion, he'd better have a blast at this one. He didn't have to fake his enjoyment of the food, though. His mom had notified the Wenches of Maverick's birth and they'd shown up laden with some of his favorite Wench-created dishes.

As the gang arrived and his mom's collie Sam rushed to greet his long-lost family, his mom took a vote. Should they start playing the games and set out dinner as a buffet folks could snack on? Or have a sit-down dinner and give their full attention to the food?

The sit-down dinner was the choice, since everyone was starving after missing lunch. Marsh and Ella ended up at the same table with his mom and Andy. Much to his embarrassment, the new grandparents spent the entire meal raving about his part in the delivery.

His mom turned to Ella. "You would have been proud of him. So kind and gentle. Jess said she wants him to deliver all her babies."

Andy smiled at him. "I can understand why she said that. You were the epitome of calm efficiency."

"Looks like I had you fooled, Andy."

"If it was an act, it was a damn good one. She was a little scared when it was just Desiree, Marybeth and me. Well, and Beau was there, but he—"

"Yeah, he was scared, all right," Ella said. "I saw that when he came out on the back porch."

"Maybe a little scared," Marsh said, "but more heartbroken than anything. He would have taken a hundred lashes if he could have spared her that pain. But once he got past blaming himself, he came through like a champ." He glanced at his mom and Andy. "You guys were awesome, too. It was a group effort."

"It was, son." His mom's gaze warmed. "But you're the one who told her to yell her head off, even swear if she wanted to. That was huge. It got her through."

"I learned that from Ella." He tipped his cider bottle in her direction.

"And I learned it from my basketball days with Coach Blake. She said there was nothing noble about suffering in silence."

"I don't think my boys have learned that." His mom looked him in the eye. "Can you honestly say you've taken that advice to heart?"

"Depends on the circumstances."

"Uh-huh. Meaning whether or not your manly pride is on the line?"

He chuckled. "Maybe."

"No maybe about it." Ella gave him a look. "Let's talk about the time you came off Pie when we were out riding and dislocated your shoulder."

"Yep." His mother nodded. "I remember hearing about that episode. Didn't you put it back on the spot?"

"I did. Learned that in basketball, too. It's not pleasant, but—"

"Are you saying he didn't yell?"

"That's what I'm saying. I told him to. I've dislocated my shoulder, so I know what it feels like. It's not a fun time." She gave him a nudge. "You were silent as the grave through the whole thing. I could hear the air hissing through his teeth, but that was it."

"I'm a slow learner." The pain had been excruciating. A best friend wouldn't have tried to impress her with his grit. But a boy who was sweet on a girl....

"You're a stubborn cowboy. But I'm glad you remembered to tell Jess, even if you wouldn't take my advice yourself."

"Next time I dislocate my shoulder I promise to turn the air blue."

"I'll believe it when I hear it."

"So, Andy." His mom switched her attention to Jess's dad. "What about you? Do you yell and cuss when you're in pain?"

"Yes, ma'am. I scream bloody murder and cry like a baby. No stiff upper lip for me."

"Then Jess's grip during the delivery wasn't painful for you?"

"Um..."

"Gotcha."

He laughed. "You didn't make any noise either, Ms. Stiff Upper Lip."

"I know. I'm teasing you. We couldn't yell. It would have upset Jess. She had no idea she was squeezing that hard."

"I had no idea she had a grip like a bronc rider. Anyway, by the time Maverick was born, my hand was numb. She'd cut off all the circulation. Couldn't feel a thing."

"Same here. Didn't mind the tingling and prickles afterward, either. We had a granddaughter. Nothing else mattered."

"Wow." Ella's expression grew wistful. "What a special, if somewhat painful, moment for you two."

"Sure was." Andy exchanged a fond glance with his mom. "Wouldn't have missed it for the world."

She smiled and touched his arm. "Me, either, Grandpa."

Andy's face lit up and he grabbed his beer bottle. "We need to toast our new status as Maverick's grandparents."

"That we do." His mother picked up her cider.

"By all means." Marsh lifted his bottle. "To Grandpa Andy and Grandma Desiree."

"Congratulations, you two." Ella tapped her bottle against the other three. "And Uncle Marsh. Let's not forget your new status."

"I don't plan to." He focused on her as he drank, and she was looking right back at him. He used to be pretty good at guessing what she was thinking. Tonight he had no clue.

* * *

Marsh would have been fine heading to his place after the meal. The suspense was killing him. But his family would wonder why he was cutting out, and Ella had sounded like she needed time to decide.

What if it was no? Could he sleep in the same house with her without going bonkers? Maybe he'd slip outside and howl at the moon whenever the strain was too much. She'd said there was nothing noble about suffering in silence.

But maybe she'd say yes. If she agreed to make love with him tonight, neither one of them would be silent. He'd see to it. Yeah, he really wanted to blow this popsicle stand.

Since he couldn't, he needed a diversion, and his mom's saloon-slash-game room had plenty of them. He helped Ella out of her chair. "Want to throw some darts?"

"Thanks, but Penny and I challenged Angie and Kendall to a game of pool."

"When was this?"

"Right after Beau announced the party was here. We had our solidarity thing going about removing our hats like guys do. Angie told Sky the four of us wanted first crack at the pool table, so he promised to reserve it for us. Put up a sign and everything." She pointed across the room.

A white piece of cardboard folded in half sat in the middle of the green felt. "I missed that."

"It says we have dibs."

"Then I'll leave you to it." He looked around for an alternative.

Bret had started a checkers game with Lucky. Checkers the size of dinner plates were lined up on the oversized board inlaid in the floor. Sam added an extra challenge by wandering across the board and sometimes sitting on one of the squares. Marsh strolled over and offered to play the winner.

"I'm already in trouble," Lucky said, "Chances are you'll play Bret, unless I get — ha, ha — *Lucky*. I'd like to blame Sam, but I can't." He scratched behind the collie's ears before picking up a checker and nudging Sam off a square so he could lay it down.

"At least we know Bret can be beaten. Kendall does it all the time."

Bret rolled his eyes. "Rub it in."

"She's a champ, all right." Lucky smiled. "I've tried to get her to give me some pointers on how she beats him, but getting engaged to Cheyenne and throwing in with Angie's handywoman business has made her a busy gal."

"I'll bet you miss hanging out with her." Marsh crouched down and coaxed Sam over so his brothers could play in peace.

"Well, sure, I do. We always had fun and she's a great dance partner. But I'm happy for her. She's been in love with Cheyenne forever. Kendall and I— we'll always be buddies. We just won't spend as much time together."

Marsh buried his fingers in Sam's ruff and gave the collie a good scratch. "Then you're not, like, upset."

Lucky made another move and Bret claimed two of his pieces. "I'm upset that Bret just got two of my guys. That's extremely upsetting."

"Don't blame me," Bret grinned. "I can't help it if you left yourself wide open. Your move."

Lucky used the toe of his boot to shove another checker forward before turning back to Marsh. "I'm not upset about Kendall, Not like you were when Ella got engaged."

"That was different." He stroked Sam's silky head. "Ella made a bad choice. You'd be upset if Kendall had picked some jerk instead of Cheyenne."

"Not upset, exactly." Lucky picked up a checker and made two jumps. "More like concerned because I like her so much. I want her to have a good life." Then he groaned as Bret made a five-point move that earned him a king.

"Okay, then I was *concerned* about Ella."

"Uh-uh, bro. You were *upset*. I mean chewing nails angry. As evidenced by the weight bench and the punching bag." His green eyes held a wisdom beyond his twenty-six years. Lucky and Rance had been born the same day but were miles apart in maturity.

Marsh dropped his gaze and focused on petting the dog. The kid saw too much. Always had, maybe because of his legacy. When his mom died in childbirth and no one claimed him, he came home with baby Rance. He'd been a McLintock since that day, but he also knew his origins were different.

"Hey." Lucky's voice grew soft. "I'm hoping it will work out for you and Ella. We're all hoping that."

Marsh glanced up. "Oh?"

"Well, yeah. You're in love with her, so we—"

"Keep it down, please." He looked around to see if anyone was in hearing distance. Specifically the lady in question.

"Everybody here knows it. Except maybe Ella, but she might, too."

"I hope to hell not."

"Why? She might be in love with you, too."

"If she was, she wouldn't have agreed to marry Stapleton."

"Good point. But that doesn't mean she *couldn't* be, sometime in the—"

"Nope. She's made her position clear for years. She loves me as a friend, but she doesn't see me as a romantic partner." But maybe she'd see him as an exciting bed partner. Better than nothing.

18

Ella hadn't needed her game face in the state championship game nearly as much as she'd needed it during the party at Rowdy Roost. She'd worked hard to ignore Marsh, but he was always in her peripheral vision — petting Sam, playing checkers with Bret, challenging Gil to a game of darts, trading jokes with Clint.

She couldn't avoid catching a glimpse of his broad shoulders or his sexy smile. The familiar sound of his laughter made her shiver with delight.

After the women had claimed their time at the pool table, Ella sat in on a poker game organized by Clint. She waited for Marsh to join in. When he didn't, she was relieved. Wasn't she?

No, she was disappointed. In herself, mostly. Why had she let him kiss her? If she'd said no, he would have backed off. And she wouldn't be fighting a losing battle with her libido.

In the years since high school, she'd never wondered what kind of lover he was. She'd never let herself think about it. Now she couldn't think about anything else.

The right of refusal still belonged to her, but his challenge flashed like neon in her brain.

Could she reject his proposition and then sleep soundly in his magnificent king-sized bed? Not a chance.

Which meant she had to go through with it, at least for tonight. Maybe it would be awful. Yeah, no. She didn't believe that for a nano-second.

He'd promised they'd have fun. He'd lit a match and she was on fire. Could anyone at this party tell? Any minute now someone would ask her why she was so distracted.

Time to get out of here before she had to tell a straight-out lie. Pleading exhaustion was easy. Keeping up appearances was hard work. She sought out Marsh.

He was in the middle of a dart game, but he handed over his darts and his winning score to Lucky immediately. Whisking them through a quick goodbye-routine, he had her out the door in no time.

The cool night air didn't do much to quench the flames licking at every inch of her body. He helped her into the truck without a word, rounded the hood in record time and swung into the driver's seat. "Well?"

"You win."

"Hot damn." He started the truck and the tires spit gravel as he backed out.

"Please don't have a wreck on the way to your place."

"Don't worry. I'm impatient, but I'm not an idiot. Besides, we have wild critters on this road at night. I'm not starting this endeavor by hitting a raccoon."

"Well said."

He pulled out on the road and, true to his word, he switched on the truck's brights and took it slow. "What tipped the balance in my favor?"

"You. No matter where I looked, there you were. Now that you've planted this audacious idea in my head, I can't stop thinking about it."

He grinned. "You never could resist an adventure."

"Damn you, no, I never can especially when you set it up so we'll have this secret from everybody. We'll get away with something outrageous, right under their noses."

"Brilliant, right?"

"Diabolical is more like it. This is still a terrible idea. I may very well regret this decision for the rest of my life, but I—"

"You won't regret it. I won't let that happen. We're going to have a great time, and at the end of it, we'll high-five each other and head off to the rest of our lives with wonderful memories of our time together."

"I'm holding you to that promise, Marsh. So help me, if we become estranged as a result of this caper, I'll never—"

"We won't. We can't. We're—"

"I know. Bulletproof."

"Damn straight. I can't imagine a future in which I'm not in regular contact with you. I don't care if you have ten kids and a jealous husband. I'll stay in touch."

His certainty warmed her in ways that had nothing to do with the sensual brew simmering in her veins. "That's lovely. But ten kids? Is that how you see my life playing out?"

"You did mention you wanted babies."

"Yeah, but not *ten.*"

"You never know. I'll bet Mom never expected to have that many."

"You said it yourself — she's a miracle of nature who gave birth easily. I'm not counting on that being the case for me."

"What number did you have in mind?"

"Two for sure. *Maybe* more, but I want to keep teaching, so two might be my limit." She glanced at him. "Kind of a strange topic for two people going off to have non-procreative sex."

"Sorry. My bad. Bottom line, whatever direction your life takes, as your best friend, I plan to be at least somewhat involved."

"Define at least somewhat."

"I'll call you twice a day."

She giggled. He got her hot, but he also made her laugh.

"Too much? Okay, once a day, then. Except on your birthday, when I'm coming over with cake and—"

"If this interlude works out, I might want you to come over for birthday sex."

"What about the jealous husband?"

"I guess he could present a problem."

"Cake it is, then." He pulled up in front of his cabin. "Indulge me tonight Ellabella. Let me come around and lift you out when you're wide awake for a change."

"And carry me to your bed?"

"You read my mind."

"Maybe you should conserve your strength, save it for later."

"Not necessary."

"Have you forgotten I'm not a small woman?"

"Have you forgotten I've been lifting weights all summer?"

"How could I, when every time I look at you, you're flexing those bulging biceps?"

"Thanks for noticing." He shut off the engine and unlatched his seat belt. "Let me show them off some more, okay? I worked hard for these manly arms."

"If you must. But it seems silly when I can let myself out."

He turned to her. "Have you got something against silly?"

Her body hummed with anticipation. "Come to think of it, no. I'm a big fan of silly."

"Excellent. I'll be around to get you and use my bulging muscles to haul you inside."

She laughed as she unbuckled her belt. "The word *haul* strikes the wrong note. You might want to use something else, like—"

"No, ma'am. I used *haul* on purpose to make you laugh. I'm going for the laugh, not the swoon." He climbed down and closed the door.

Huh. So this was what sex for the fun of it looked like. Definitely different. She'd never—

He yanked her door open. "Let's go."

"Geez, that was fast."

"I'm in a hurry." He was panting.

"You ran around the truck?"

"I did. Duck your head."

"Okay. Since I was asleep the other times, I don't know how you— hey!" She squealed in protest as he pulled her out and tossed her neatly over his shoulder. "What do you think you're—"

"Hauling you inside. Be quiet. You'll wake the neighbors."

"You have no neighbors." The blood rushed to her head as she dangled upside down. Great view of his tempting buns, though. Within reach, too. Touching was allowed, now, wasn't it? She pinched him as hard as she could through the denim.

"Ow!"

"That was so much fun." She reached for him again.

"Lay off my ass, lady."

"Why should I? You put me in this position, so I— ouch!" She yelled for effect. His gentle pinch didn't hurt in the least, but it sure sent a potent message to her hoo-ha.

"Wuss. That didn't hurt." He climbed the porch steps. He was puffing, but he didn't slow down.

"How do you know?"

"You're tougher than that. I barely squeezed. Your fingers are like vise grips." Crossing the porch, he opened the front door.

"If you didn't want me to pinch you, you shouldn't have—"

"Oh, I like being pinched. Just not that hard."

"You like being pinched?

"Yes, ma'am. And so do you." He walked into the dark living room, kicked the door shut and kept going, striding purposefully down the hall. "Just go easy next time."

"You're planning to repeat this maneuver?"

"I might. I kinda like it."

"Is this how you treat ladies?"

"Only when the sex is just for fun." Carrying her into the inky blackness of his room, he kept going until his knee bumped into the mattress. Then he dropped his shoulder and let her slide off.

She tumbled onto the cushy surface. "I can't see a thing."

"Ever done it in total darkness?"

"Nope." The sound of his husky voice coming from the shadows brought her nipples to a taut peak.

"Me, either." One of his boots thumped to the floor, followed by the second one. "If we move fast, we'll be into it before our eyes adjust." Snaps popped as he wrenched open his shirt.

"I like that idea." Breathing fast, she pulled off her boots and dropped them over the side of the bed at the same time his belt buckle clanked as it hit the wooden floor. "You're..." She gulped in air. "Way ahead of me."

"I need to be. I'm on condom duty and you're not."

Her core clenched. This was happening. No turning back, now. His instincts were on target with this darkness routine, though. If they couldn't see each other, she could pretend she was having sex with a complete stranger.

She wiggled out of her clothes and threw everything on the floor on the other side of the bed.

Wood scraped when he opened the bedside table drawer. "Did you look in here today?"

Not a stranger. Only Marsh would ask her that. "Of course I did."

"Do you approve of my brand?" Foil crinkled.

She peered in the direction of the sound. He was in shadows, but objects were starting to become more defined. "It's a decent kind." Her voice sounded funny. Too high-pitched. If the faint image of his package her brain had delivered was accurate....

"Move over. I'm coming in."

She scooted to the other side of the bed.

"Not that far." He climbed in, making the quilt rustle.

"Can you see me?" Heart jackhammering in her chest, she eased back in his direction.

"Sort of. I can hear you breathing, though. And I can smell you."

"Marsh! A gentleman does *not* say such—"

"Aroused woman. My favorite smell." He loomed over her, blocking what little bit of starlight had seeped in through the window.

"Better hurry. I can almost see your face."

"This should help." Leaning down, he touched his mouth to hers, lightly at first, as if to make sure he was in the right place. Then he settled in, his kiss surprisingly tender.

Grasping his head, she slackened her jaw and took it up a notch. His breathing changed and he plunged his tongue deep.

That opened the floodgates, sending moisture rushing to places that ached for his touch. When she moaned, he nudged her thighs apart and trailed one hand from her throat all the way to her quivering stomach. Then lower.

Lifting his head, he caressed her with deliberate intent, his fingers going where she'd never guessed they ever would. "This is it, Ellabella."

Her body throbbed in anticipation. "Go for it."

He took her at her word. One firm thrust and they were joined as they'd never been before.

The shadows hadn't lied. Neither had the promise made by the bulge in his Jockeys.

"Ella? You okay?"

She gulped, dazed by the pleasure, the snug fit, the absolute rightness of Marsh between her thighs. "I'm fine. Great." She dragged in a breath. "I just need a moment."

_19_

Marsh heaved a sigh of relief. "I was worried that you... weren't happy."

"I'm extremely happy." Ella reached up and stroked his cheek. "But this is trippy."

"No kidding." He gazed down at her. "I can see your eyes. They're kind of sparkly."

"I feel like I'm sparkly all over."

He smiled. "Are you going all _Twilight_ on me?" Bracing himself on his forearms, he raised up a little so he could take his first look at Ella, naked. He couldn't see much, but what he could see was promising. "Sorry to say this, but you're not sparkly."

"I didn't say I _was._ I said I felt like it."

"In other words, you're having a good time with this turn of events?"

"So far. You're very well-endowed."

"Thank you."

"You can't take credit for it, Marsh. It's in your genes."

"Most of the time it's in my jeans. Currently it's in your—"

"I know exactly where it is, smart aleck."

"I take it you like having it there."

"Now you're fishing."

"Yes, ma'am."

"I'm reserving judgment."

"Why is that?"

"Just because you were blessed with super-sized equipment doesn't mean you know how to use it."

He laughed. "Seriously? You're tossing down the gauntlet?"

"Yes. Yes, I am." She gripped his ass. "Show me what you've got, cowboy."

Ella's hands on his butt and her saucy challenge were a powerful combo. As a member of a rambunctious family, he'd learned early to fight for what he wanted.

And he wanted Ella. But he refused to perform like a trained dog to win the blue ribbon. Lowering his head, he nibbled on her plump lips. "This is a two-person exercise. You'll need to show me what you've got, too, y'know. You can't just lie there and collect orgasms."

Her soft chuckle warmed his lips. "Don't worry. I'm a participator. If you don't start moving, I will."

"I'm tempted to let you take the reins." He eased back a little and pushed in deep. Her gasp of reaction did his heart good. It did his cock even more good. "But I'm not gonna."

He began slowly. They'd rushed to get to this point and they'd accomplished it, broken through the barrier created by years of a platonic relationship. Time to collect the rewards.

Each gradual thrust built the tension. Her fingers dug into his glutes and she lifted her hips to meet him on the downstroke, creating that vital connection that would make her a very happy woman.

It wouldn't take long. Her steady breathing became soft little gasps. The warm, tight channel that cradled him began to flex.

Joy rose within him as he anticipated the moment when she'd let go, when her cries of release would fill him with more pleasure than he could hold. Almost there. He pumped faster, unearthing her secrets, yearning for a response that would eclipse every moment they'd ever shared.

Now. *Now.* He pushed in, drew back, pushed hard once more and she arched into him, seeking that exquisite pressure that set off the rockets. He bore down and she came, loudly, enthusiastically, and most precious of all, calling his name.

He drank it in — the undulations rolling over his cock, her trembling thighs, her mewling cries as the orgasm claimed her, stripping away all pretense, every subtle barrier that had stood between them.

At long last, he'd touched the essence of the woman he loved.

Panting, she dug the tips of her fingers into his butt. "Now you." She was hoarse from celebrating her climax, but insistent. "You know you want to."

The mere suggestion nearly did the trick. He clenched his jaw against the urge. "If I don't..." He dragged in air. "I can give you another—"

"But..." Her voice grew soft. "Then I'm the only one who's... you know."

Vulnerable. "I do know." He began to stroke, fast and hard. "Won't take long."

"Ooo, I like this." She cupped his glutes as she kept pace with him. "Nice muscles here, too." She gave him a squeeze.

He gasped as the pressure built. "Thanks." Ella could move like no one he'd ever— *ahhh.*

"Did you just growl?"

"Mm." Close, now. Very close.

"Must feel great."

"You have... no idea." He plunged deep and erupted with a shout of triumph. *Yes!* Dear God, yes, yes, YES. As he gasped for air, he gazed down, needing to make sure this was real, that Ella was lying there beneath him.

She most certainly was. Even without any light except the stars shining faintly through the bedroom window, he could make out her sweet, tender smile.

She touched his cheek. "It's you, and yet it's not you. Does that make any sense?"

"No."

"When you threw yourself into it, you sounded so primitive, so elemental."

"Felt that way, too." Could explain his snap decision to toss her over his shoulder.

"I wondered, who is this guy?"

"Did I scare you? I wouldn't want to—"

"Heck, no. It was thrilling, discovering that unknown side. But then you yelled like the time you hit the game-winning home run senior year, and you were back to being the person I've known most of my life."

But not like this. Gradually his heartbeat steadied and he took a deep breath. "That climax with you was ten times better than any home run, ever."

"Yeah?"

"Oh, yeah." Leaning down, he gave her a soft kiss. "But I knew it would be."

"How could you be sure?"

"Weren't you?"

"Yes. I'd seen how your girlfriends look at you."

"Then why did you imply I wouldn't know what to do with my attributes?"

"Just messing with you."

"Oh, really?" He pushed up and balanced on one arm so he had his other hand free. There was a spot right below her ribcage, a little above her waistline. He made a move toward it.

"Don't you dare!" She grabbed his wrist. "Don't you dare tickle me, Marsh McLintock!"

She was no match for him, not after weeks of training. "You can't stop me."

"Ohhh, you don't want to say that, Marsh."

He stilled as she took hold of his family jewels, one of them, anyway. While he'd been concentrating on her tickle zone, she'd bent her knee to the side and made her countermove. Long arms had helped make her a star. And a worthy opponent in the tickle wars.

She squeezed just enough to get her point across. "Give?"

"You're bluffing."

"Am I?"

"You'll be sorry if you damage the merchandise and wreck our plans for the evening."

"You'll be sorry if you tickle me and dislodge your condom."

He started laughing.

"What's so funny?"

"Same *you'll be sorry* game. Radically different stakes."

"Oh, my God, Marsh. We haven't changed a bit! That's embarrassing."

"Gonna let go?"

"Gonna promise not to tickle me?"

"Yes. Let go of me and I'll take care of this condom before it becomes a problem."

"You're free to go."

"Thanks." With a firm grip on the condom, he withdrew. "I'll be back."

"Back in the room or back in my—"

"Both." He left the bed. "We still have major fooling around to do."

"Tomorrow's a workday for you."

"I know." He headed for the attached bath, one he'd purposely designed to give him plenty of room. He flipped on a light so he could see what he was doing and avoid knocking over any of Ella's lotions and potions.

"You said you're busy this week."

"I might have moved a couple of routine physicals I had scheduled for tomorrow." After disposing of the condom, he walked over to the sink and soaped up a washcloth. Ella's stuff lined up neatly on a shelf looked domestic and cozy.

"Meaning?"

"I gave myself tomorrow off." He cleaned his happy bad boy. Might as well start the rest of this promising night fresh.

"I invited Faye to come out for lunch."

"Great! Can't wait to see her." He grabbed a towel and dried off.

"You mentioned keeping our activities a secret. Faye will know instantly."

"Then we should tell her." He hung up the towel, walked back toward the door and reached to turn off the light. Changed his mind. Since the door was opposite the end of the bed, if he left the light on, they'd have some illumination. Might be time.

"Tell her what, exactly?"

"The truth." He walked out of the bathroom. Ella was sitting up facing him, and the glow from the bathroom provided a better view than he'd counted on. Whatever he'd been about to say vanished. He stared in reverent silence at the blonde goddess in his bed.

She was equally wide-eyed. Her gaze traveled slowly downward, lingering on his pride and joy long enough to achieve lift-off.

He cleared his throat. "If the light upsets you, I can turn it off."

"I'm not upset." She made the return journey and looked him straight in the eye. "And I don't want to waste time talking about my sister."

20

After experiencing Marsh's gifts up close and personal, Ella had taken the measure of the man in the most intimate way possible. Getting a visual in better light should be anticlimactic, right?

Wrong. So wrong. Logically, her view of him this morning in his Jockeys should have prepared her for the full monty. It had not. She'd been missing the most magnificent piece to the puzzle.

She had plenty of time to ogle as he stood backlit by the golden glow coming from the bathroom. He'd frozen in place the minute he'd caught sight of her. Well, most of him had frozen. His midsection was gearing up, clearly going rogue.

She said the first thing that came to her. "You should never wear clothes."

His dazed expression morphed into an amused one. "I won't if you won't."

"Deal. At least until we're forced to be around other people."

"Like your sister." He approached the bed.

"The person I don't want to take time to discuss because... because..." She started to giggle and gestured toward his fully erect cock.

"I had nothing to do with that."

"I can tell." She swallowed a burst of laughter. "You know what a witching stick is?"

"Yes, I do, and you don't have to explain the reference."

"It's like—" She cleared the laughter from her throat. "Like it's leading you to me."

He deadpanned his response. "That's exactly right. My witching dick wants what it wants. I just go in the direction it's pointing and pray I find water."

She lost it, laughing so hard she got the hiccups.

"Told you we'd have fun."

Wiping the tears from her eyes, she tossed back the covers and swung her feet to the floor, hiccupping the whole time. "I need to get rid of these."

"I kinda hate to see them go. I haven't been treated to this much jiggle since binge-watching reruns of *Baywatch*."

"You're terrible." She motioned to him. "Come over here. I have an idea."

He walked around the side of the bed. "If you're thinking sex can cure hiccups, my buddy's on board with that and I'm willing to go along for the ride."

"That might work, but I have something different in mind."

"We're listening."

She rolled her eyes. "Next you'll tell me you've named him."

"No, ma'am. Sooner or later I'd meet someone with that name. Just my luck it'd be my future father-in-law."

"Wise choice. Especially considering my hiccup recovery plan." Excitement tasted like champagne on her tongue. Even if this didn't work, she'd longed to do it ever since he'd walked out of the bathroom.

His eyes narrowed. "Are you thinking what I think you're thinking?"

"Come closer and you'll find out."

"You *are* thinking what I think you're thinking. I know that look."

"How could you? We've never done this."

"It's the look you get when your banana split arrives."

"Excellent comparison."

He edged backward "With the hiccups? What if you bite me?"

"I won't. Where's your spirit of adventure?"

"How about if I get you a glass of water? After your hiccups are gone, then—"

"Admit it. You're a big fat chicken." She had to fit the words around her hiccups. "What if it's even better with those little jolts? What if it's the ultimate blow job?" She locked her gaze with his and ran her tongue over her lips. Hiccups kept it from being a totally smooth move.

Still effective, though. He sucked in a breath and his cock twitched. "Okay." He stepped within reach. "Be careful, please."

"I promise." Her pulse skittered like water on a hot skillet as she wrapped her fingers around the most electrifying thing she'd touched in ages. She glanced up.

He'd closed his eyes and clenched his jaw. His chest heaved and his skin quivered, setting in motion the fine hairs sprinkled over his impressive pecs.

"Scared?"

He shook his head. "Sensitive."

Moisture pooled in her mouth. This amazing specimen of manhood had been there all along — sitting next to her on the couch watching movies, across the table eating burgers at the Buns and Beer, spinning her around the dance floor on a Saturday night. If he hadn't talked her into this escapade, her ignorance would have continued forever.

She leaned forward and swiped her tongue over the velvet tip.

He groaned.

"I guess you are sensitive."

"Didn't think I would be. Not after we talked it to death."

"You talked it to death. I've never had to convince a guy—"

"Never mind." He dragged in air. "Just go easy."

"Sure thing." She didn't go very far at first. Sliding her lips over his considerable girth caused her nether parts to quickly become slippery and achy. With the first hiccup, she instinctively took him deeper.

He swore softly and clutched her head.

Would he make her stop? She waited for one beat, two beats. Another hiccup and she added more territory.

Another string of soft curses. His fingertips pressed into her scalp, but not hard enough to hurt.

When she added gentle suction, the swearing got slightly louder, and adding hiccups to the mix brought out some words she'd never heard him use. His grip on her scalp tightened slightly and his breathing roughened to the point of panting.

Another hiccup. And another. She slackened her jaw and moved even lower until the tip of his cock touched the back of her throat. One more hiccup.

"Ella, I can't... I'm...." His body shook. Chanting the F-word, he came.

And she swallowed. And swallowed some more. And took the last of it as he trembled and gulped for air.

"Didn't mean to." His breathy words were hard to catch. "Tried to hold back." He lightly massaged her scalp. "Felt... too... good."

Easing away slowly, she gazed upward. "Glad you liked it."

"Loved it." Grasping her by the shoulders, he drew her to her feet and gave her a kiss of gratitude that left her gasping for breath. He lifted his mouth a fraction from hers. "Hiccups gone?"

"All gone. Next time I get the hiccups, I know where to go for help."

"Glad I could be of service." He nibbled his way down the curve of her neck and along one shoulder. "Although if it happens again, we should test my remedy."

"What's that?"

"I'll show you when the time comes." He nipped her shoulder and kissed his way back to her mouth, outlining her lips with the tip of his tongue.

"It's something sexual, isn't it?"

"You could say that. Want me to show you?"

"What do you think? Of course."

He cupped her face and gazed into her eyes. "Act like you have the hiccups."

"Do I have to? Can't you just—"

"Work with me, here. Make that little hitching noise in your throat. Do it every couple of seconds. It's important to the concept."

"No, it's not. Quit teasing me and just do it."

He grinned. "You used to be easier to fool."

"Some might say I'm still easily fooled."

His grin disappeared and he wrapped her in his arms, tugging her close, his face inches from hers. "But you're not."

"I am, so. I believed he was a good guy who wanted the same things I did."

"Because he's an expert at what he does. He's learned how to take a person's dream and twist it to his advantage."

"I should have seen through him. When he insisted on flying in on the morning of the wedding, I should have realized that he—"

"You were just trying to hang onto your dream, Ellabella." He leaned his forehead against hers. "You don't need a hiccup cure. But you desperately need a cure to get that bastard out of your head. I'm going to make you forget all about him."

"That sounds lovely. Every time I think of how easily I was duped, I..." She sucked in a breath and drew back. "Oh, no."

"Ella?"

"What if I said yes to this adventure because I needed you to soothe my battered ego?"

"What if you did?"

"That's so selfish."

"Not from where I stand. You didn't ask me. I asked you."

"To get me through a tough time?"

"I'm not that noble. I asked because I wanted to share this experience and we'd never have a better opportunity. If it helps heal your battered ego, so much the better. After all, that's what friends are for."

_21_

Guiding Ella down to the broad expanse of his bed, Marsh paid homage to the woman he'd loved for most of his life. He followed his instincts, a light touch here, a firm one there, an open-mouthed kiss on the plump surface of her satin breast, a swipe of his tongue across her taut nipple.

His instincts must be on target. She arched into his caresses with enthusiasm and urged him on with happy sighs and heartfelt moans. By the time he'd kissed his way to her inner thigh, she was so ready to fall in with his plans.

He nuzzled his way into the sweet center of all things Ella and loved her until she came. And came again.

As she lay panting, her arms flung out and her body limp, he scooted up, plucked a condom from the drawer and put it on. He brushed a kiss over her lips. "Mind if I join the party?"

Her eyes widened. "Really? So soon?"

"You inspire me."

"Careful, you're moving into superhero territory."

"I don't think they have sex."

"Well, if they did, it would be exactly like this."

He smiled. "Only better, because I don't have to leave you craving more sex while I chase after the bad guys."

"What a relief." She held out her arms. "Come join the party. Stay as long as you want."

How about forever? He swallowed, hit with a tsunami of yearning that threatened to give him away. "Watch who you say that to. You could end up with some bozo you can't get rid of. "

"Yeah, but I can say it to you. You'll never take advantage." Her blue eyes glowed with happiness, courtesy of two orgasms from someone she trusted.

"I never will." He let his eager cock have what it wanted, allowing it to sink effortlessly into Ella's lush warmth. He didn't mean to groan. The sound escaped before he could close his throat, holding it back.

She hugged him. "I'm so happy you like this."

He pushed up on his arms so he could meet her gaze. "Let me be clear. I love this."

"Me, too. Great plan."

"What plan?" When he was this close to paradise, his brain went on vacay.

"Some sexual fun before we move on with our lives."

If only she hadn't included the phrase *before we move on with our lives,* he'd be thrilled with her comment. He should be thrilled with it, though. He'd billed the idea exactly that way. He hadn't specifically said *before we move on*, but it was implied. Probably one reason she'd agreed.

To hell with it. He was right where he wanted to be, as close as he could get to the woman of his dreams. Better yet, the light in her blue eyes told him she wanted him there. She cherished the connection.

She squeezed him tighter. "Are you gonna move?"

He smiled. "Yes." Because that was the idea, and yet striving for his climax wasn't his goal. Hadn't been since the moment they'd climbed into this bed together.

Sure, he wanted her to have them, wanted her to be sexually satisfied as a result of this maneuver. But once he'd made this special connection, his needs were met.

"You're still not moving." She wiggled her hips.

"Thinking." She'd never been more beautiful — her blonde hair spread out on the pillow, her skin flushed pink from his loving.

"You've always been a thinker, Marsh. That's part of your problem."

"Thinking's a problem?"

"Right now it is."

"Yes, ma'am." Easing back, he thrust forward. And again, and again, glorying in her quick response, the way her eyes darkened to navy and her breath caught. They'd always been physically in sync. And never more than in this bed.

She gave a cute little nod of approval. "That's better."

His chuckle was a little ragged. "Glad you approve."

"Mm, yessir," she crooned softly. "I surely dooo..." She gasped. "What did you—"

"Shifted..." He sucked in air as she tightened her core muscles. "...the angle."

"Keep doing that."

"Believe I will."

Her breathing picked up speed. "I think... we can... come together."

He moved faster, eased up on his control. "Yes, ma'am."

"I'm close, now."

He gulped. "Me, too."

"Now, Marsh. *Now.*"

Her first spasm triggered his. He let go, a guttural cry wrenched from deep in his chest as he pushed deep.

With a wild cry, she abandoned herself to her release. He groaned as her climax rolled over his pulsing cock, magnifying the shock waves that spread from his groin to every nerve firing in his quivering body.

Time expanded, each second so full of pleasure that he lost track of how long he stayed propped on his elbows gazing into her eyes. Those blue depths gleamed with the same awe that filled his chest and tightened his throat.

At last she took a quick breath and ran her tongue over her bottom lip. "That was..." She paused. "I don't have a word for it."

"There isn't one."

"You're right. I thought... I thought it would just be cool to try. I didn't... it was way more..." She sighed. "I give up."

He smiled and leaned down to give her a soft kiss. "We don't have to describe it. We lived it."

"Of course I want to try it again."

He lifted his head. "Now?"

"Not now, silly. We should quit while we're ahead."

"Meaning?"

"My guess is we can't top that, not considering how late it must be. It's likely downhill from here."

"Downhill? Since when did you become such a pessimist?"

"Be honest. Aren't you a little bit sleepy?"

"I will neither confirm nor deny."

"That settles it. You're exhausted."

"I didn't—"

"Whenever you give me that *neither confirm nor deny* line, it's because the answer is *hell, yes*, but you can't admit it and you don't want to lie."

"Going to sleep seems so lame. There's nothing exciting or adventurous about it."

"Okay, if you won't admit you're tired, I will. We didn't get much sleep last night, so we both should be running on fumes."

"I'm not, but—"

"You're out of fumes?"

"I'm fine, smarty-pants, but if you're tired, that's a whole different story."

"You tell yourself that if that's what it takes."

"I do hate to move from this most excellent spot, though."

"I understand. I like you there, too, but eventually, shrinkage—"

"Point taken." He reluctantly shifted away from her, missing the connection immediately, and climbed out of bed. "I'll take care of this and be back. I'll shut off the light on my way out of the bathroom so you can sleep."

"Yes, by all means, do it for me. You can stay awake and watch over me."

"I probably will."

"I'm so sure." She snickered. "I believe I've heard this exchange a few times before."

"Like when?" He walked into the bathroom and took care of business.

"Like the time we rode into the mountains and it started to snow and you'd forgotten your gloves and kept telling me your hands were fine, but we needed to turn around because clearly I was freezing."

"You were freezing." He washed up quickly. "You were shivering."

"Shaking with laughter is more like it. You were so funny, absolutely determined to show me how strong and manly you were even if you lost a finger to frostbite."

"I'm lucky I didn't." The evidence kept piling up. He might have called her his best friend all these years, but he'd been stuck on her since... shoot, maybe the whole time.

Turning off the bathroom light, he started back into the bedroom.

"Would you turn that back on for a minute, please?"

"Sure." He flicked it on again as she climbed out of bed, all five feet, ten inches of gorgeous female.

"I need a pit stop before we call it a night." She smiled as she walked past him with her long-legged stride. "Nature calls." Stepping inside, she closed the door.

They'd shared a bathroom many times when they'd met at his house or hers to watch movies. But tonight was different. Instead of watching movies, they'd had sex. And would crawl into the same bed, naked, to get some shut-eye.

Not so different from being married, was it? And he liked it. Wanted it. He'd be a fool to say that now, but he would say it eventually. He'd take the chance on creating an awkwardness that never went away.

The toilet flushed, followed by water running in the sink. When she didn't come out right away, he paid attention to the muted sounds coming from behind the closed door. "Are you brushing your teeth?"

"I am. So what?"

"If you're brushing, I'm brushing."

"Copycat."

"I'll get my brush and toothpaste from the guest bath."

"Suit yourself. I had a piece of Nancy's Death by Chocolate cake and that thing's delicious, but it's loaded with sugar."

He grinned. She'd been a dedicated brusher and flosser since grade school. She'd hung on to that endearing habit and it made him happy that she had.

Damn it, he knew this woman. He'd be an excellent choice for her. But she had a blind spot when it came to that concept. He didn't understand it, but discussing it with her would unmask him.

He couldn't risk that, not when this adventure was so new. He'd look for clues in the next few days and especially in the next few nights. He was counting on those nights to make a lasting impression, an activity she couldn't easily give up.

22

Ella rolled over and came up against a warm, solid body. She gasped. Oh. Right. Marsh. Sexiest man alive.

He gave her a sleepy smile and tugged her closer. "Morning, Ellabella."

"Then I didn't dream it." A mishmash of anxiety and excitement danced in her stomach.

"No, ma'am, it's real."

Too real. A flush spread over her skin. They were no longer under cover of darkness. Desire simmered, making her edgy. Last night's bonfire had incinerated her inhibitions. Morning light had reawakened them.

He frowned. "You don't look exactly happy about that."

"I'm not *un*happy. It's just... last night it was dark in here, and even when you turned on the bathroom light, it wasn't like this. It wasn't sunny."

"If you think this is sunny, you should try waking up in my guest room. The sun hits that window and bam, you're awake or else."

"It's plenty bright in here, too."

His frown deepened. "But you love sunshine. Summer's your favorite time of year because there's so much—"

"I do love it."

"Which begs the question, why are you uneasy now that the sun's up?"

"I'm not exactly—"

"Yes, you are. It's like you weren't prepared to wake up in this bed with me. And you're uncomfortable with the idea."

"I'm a little bit discombobulated. It's not like I don't remember making the choice."

His eyebrows lifted.

"And the great sex that followed."

His expression relaxed and his gaze warmed. "It was great. Amazing."

"And it seemed natural to just let go. But this morning..."

"Not so natural?"

"Not really."

"Tell you what." He released her and climbed out of bed. "I'll go start some coffee and evaluate our choices for breakfast. I meant to stock up yesterday, but things got a little—"

"Crazy. No worries. Faye is bringing provisions." She sat up and glanced at the digital clock on the nightstand. "She'll be here in less than two hours, so maybe we shouldn't eat a whole lot." She wasn't ready to face her sister, yet. This was all so new. But canceling wasn't an option.

"Why is she bringing food? I have a fridge full of it, and things in the freezer." He picked up his briefs and put them on without a hint of self-consciousness.

"I asked her to bring a few things from the market because I didn't want to be a mooch." A glimpse of Marsh's toned body gave her a strong hint as to why she'd fallen right into bed with him last night and been very happy to stay there.

"A mooch? You're the least moochy person I know." He pulled up his jeans, fastened the button and zipped his fly. Shooting her a quick glance, he chuckled. "Ella, you're staring at my crotch."

"Oh! No, I'm not, not really. I was just—"

"Remembering?"

She met his amused gaze. Certain parts of her remembered exceedingly well. The tug of arousal kicked up her heart rate.

Amusement shifted to something much hotter. He reached for the button of his jeans. "Maybe we need to stay in bed a little longer."

"No." She quickly swung her feet to the floor and stood. "I'll head for the shower." She moved past him, avoiding any accidental body contact. "And thanks for offering to make coffee. I would love some. Coffee sounds terrific."

"Want me to bring it to you?"

"No, thanks. I'll come out and get it once I'm dressed." She closed the bathroom door and gulped in air.

What was wrong with her? Last night she'd been all in, ready for anything. Now she was having the worst case of morning-after jitters she'd ever experienced.

Did she regret last night? No, not a single second of it. She'd never enjoyed sex more. Clearly her eager body wanted more of the same. So why had she run away like a scared rabbit?

She'd likely confused the hell out of Marsh. That wasn't fair. He'd just given her the most spectacular night of her life and now she was acting weird.

Grabbing one of his generously large bath towels, she wrapped up in it and padded barefoot out of the bedroom, down the hall, through the living room and into the kitchen. "Marsh."

He glanced up from measuring coffee into the basket. "Hey, there. Don't tell me the hot water heater's on the fritz. I just had it—"

"I apologize for acting like a lunatic just now."

"You got the yips. It happens."

"That's possible." She took a breath. "Or the bends might be more accurate. Too deep, too fast."

He turned away from the coffee pot and leaned his hips against the counter. "If there's something I can do, or not do, just tell me."

"Put on a shirt?"

"Says the woman who's wearing a towel."

"I felt the need to come out immediately and say something instead of leaving you wondering what the—"

"I know. I'm teasing. Want me to go get my shirt?"

She sighed. "That would be ridiculous after what happened last night."

"Ridiculous or not, I'll cover up if that helps the cause."

"I should be able to talk to you when you're bare-chested. We've gone swimming together since we were kids."

"Yeah, but we're not kids, anymore."

"And you bulked up this summer, which doesn't help."

He grinned. "Sorry, not sorry."

"The truth is, I can't look at you, dressed or undressed, without thinking about having sex. And I don't... I don't know how to handle that."

"It'll wear off."

"Doesn't feel like it. I've been with guys before. I never felt this level of... craving."

He swallowed. "On second thought, maybe we should both get dressed."

"Okay." She started out of the kitchen. "I'll grab that shower and put on clothes," she called over her shoulder. "Lots of clothes."

"Wait." He came after her. "I have a better idea."

"If it's going back to bed, I—"

"It's not. Did you bring sweats?"

"Yes."

"And a T-shirt?"

"Sure."

"Then why don't you put those on before you take that shower and I'll teach you how to use the punching bag."

Her eyes widened. "That's *brilliant*."

"Thank you."

"Seriously, that's a perfect idea. I talked with Angie last night and she's more than happy to loan me her gloves."

"I figured she would be."

"I don't know why I didn't think of this myself."

"Then go get dressed and I'll meet you on the back porch."

She started down the hall. "Don't you need some clothes from your room?"

"I transferred my workout clothes to the guest room." He followed behind her. "I'll dress in there. See you on the back porch."

"Can I just wear my running shoes?"

"Depends on whether you want to try kickboxing, too."

She spun around so fast they almost collided. "Kickboxing? You've learned how?"

"Taught myself by watching videos online. Figured I might as well, since I invested in the bag."

"I've always wanted to learn that, too. I wish I'd known what you were up to. Maybe we could have—"

"You were up to your eyeballs in wedding plans."

She made a face. "What a waste of valuable time *that* was. Meanwhile you bought a punching bag and taught yourself kickboxing."

"Yeah, but now I can teach you, at least as much as I know. You'll catch on fast."

"Then no shoes?"

"No shoes. There's a mat to protect your tender tootsies. See you in a few." He ducked into the guest room and closed the door.

What a good friend. He hadn't closed that door because he was shy. He'd done it out of respect for her sudden attack of nerves. He was both sweet *and* sexy.

She put on her sweats and an old Wagon Train High T-shirt. Locating a scrunchie, she put her hair in a ponytail and set off for the back porch.

He'd left the back door open and was already out there taking a few bare-knuckled jabs at the bag hanging from a rafter. His workout clothes were gray sweats and a black muscle shirt that showed off his pecs and biceps to perfection.

He hadn't heard her arrive, which gave her a chance to admire his bulging muscles as he attacked the bag. God, he was beautiful. Gradually the tightness that had plagued her since waking up in his bed loosened. Warmth pooled low in her belly.

A session with the punching bag would be fun. A quick romp in bed after they finished would be even more fun. He'd cured her case of the yips.

23

When Marsh settled into a punching routine, he zoned out, one of the big benefits of the exercise. But Ella's quick intake of breath, coming between blows, penetrated his concentration and he turned.

Hot damn. He was liking that gleam in her eyes. He'd started punching just to have something to do, but if it had achieved more than that, bonus. "Ready to get started?" *Ready for more than that?*

"Yes." She smiled. "You look like you're having a blast. I can't wait to try."

"Warmups first." He moved away from the bag. "I start with twenty jumping jacks, then do a few arm rotations and a couple of forward bends."

"Got it." She moved into position about five feet away, facing him. "One, two, three, *go.*"

He synchronized his jumps to hers. They used to do exercise routines on a regular basis before Stapleton threw a monkey wrench into their friendship.

Ella clearly loved movement. She grinned with happiness, her ponytail swinging in time with her jumps. He'd missed her like the devil.

They quit at precisely the same moment, which made her laugh. "Like old times, huh?"

"Yes, ma'am. Now do ten windmills."

"I make my classes warm up before we do any of the fun stuff. They mostly hate warming up."

"Because they're young and impatient. We used to hate it, too."

"But now we're old and patient?"

"Older and wiser."

"That's debatable." She let her arms drop to her sides. "Forward bend." She flopped over, supple as a willow branch.

And he wanted that supple body in his arms, in his bed, writhing with pleasure as he—

"Marsh. Forward bend."

"Yes, ma'am." He leaned into the stretch.

"Lost you for a minute, there. Bet you were thinking."

"I was." He straightened.

"Want to share?"

"No, ma'am." He walked over to a shelf and took down his gloves and Angie's, plus the hand wraps. "I'd rather teach you how to use this bag."

"I'll need help with the gloves. I know nothing about how to—"

"Got you covered." Laying both sets of gloves and his hand wraps on the mat at his feet, he gave her one of Angie's wraps. "I'll do your right hand and let you do the left. It's not complicated. Hold your hand out with your wrist straight."

She stretched her hand toward him, fingers flexing, and damned if he didn't flash back to those same fingers wrapped around his cock.

That part of his anatomy began to swell. He took a deep breath.

"Are you okay?" She peered at him. "Your face is a little flushed."

"It's warm out here." Giving a stern warning to his cock, he wrapped her hand and narrated the process so she'd be ready to wrap her left one. By the time he secured the Velcro tab, he was back in control.

"Simple enough."

"I'll put mine on while you're wrapping your left hand. Holler if you get confused." He moved out of the temptation zone.

She was worried about her fixation on sex, but his was just as troublesome. Working with the punching bag might diffuse the tension, but he wasn't counting on it.

"I'm done. Ready for the gloves."

He inspected her job. "Nice. I had a hunch you'd take to this."

"That's a no-brainer. If it appeals to you, chances are good it will appeal to me. Glove me up, please."

"I'll put both on this time, because it's awkward at first." He moved fast. The sooner they started punching, the less likely he'd try to kiss her. "Flex your fingers. Tell me how it feels."

"Like I could knock Warner into the middle of next week."

He laughed. "Is that where we're going with this?"

"You doubted it? Although you'd probably rather not picture your beloved punching bag as Warner Stapleton the Third."

"Why not? I've been doing it all summer."

Her gaze met his in silent understanding. "Then let's join forces and beat the crap out of him."

"Yes, ma'am." He put on his gloves. "First rule, keep your hands up." He held both gloves close to this face. "Keep your wrist straight when you punch and hit the bag with your knuckles." He extended his arm and glanced at her. "No floppy wrists. You could hurt yourself."

She nodded. "I get the concept."

"As soon as you throw a punch, bring that hand right back to the same position."

"Let me see you hit the bag."

He demonstrated, planting his fist smack-dab in Warner's face. Then he began a shuffle step, gloves up. "Some instructors advise staying basically in the same place, but I like to move around, get Warner swinging and then punch him from a different direction."

"You actually call this bag Warner?"

"Sometimes. Other times I have more colorful names for him."

"I wanna see how you kick him in the nuts."

He flashed her a grin. "Bloodthirsty, are you?"

"You know it, buster."

"Then here we go." He demonstrated a jab, a cross and a round kick with his right leg.

"I love it. I want to learn that combo so I can imagine planting my foot in his—"

"You kick the bag with your shin, not your foot."

"My shin? How am I supposed to make contact with his privates if I'm using my shin?"

"You can't. If that's your goal—"

"My fantasy. I don't believe in seeking revenge, but pretending I'm whaling on him, that's fun."

"Then your fantasy requires a push kick. Lead into it like this — jab, cross, jab, push kick." He finished the routine with his leg straight out in front of him. "Use the ball of your foot, not the entire bottom of it."

"Looks effective. And appropriate, using the ball of your foot."

He glanced at her. "Promise me you're not going to—"

"I'm not plotting to lure him into a back alley and unload my new kickboxing moves on him, if that's what you're thinking."

"You have that look in your eye."

"Probably because I wish I'd smacked him Saturday morning in the heat of the moment."

"That makes two of us."

"He had it coming."

"He probably still does, but—"

"Launching an unprovoked attack is unworthy. It's not who we are."

"Exactly." He stepped away from the bag and took off his gloves. "Try a few punches, see how it feels. I suggest starting slow with some easy jabs. Develop a rhythm, get comfortable with the process before you go hammer and tongs."

"Excellent advice." Her mouth tilted up. "For lots of things."

"Oh?" Devil woman. He pretended innocence as he unwound his hand wraps. "Like what?"

"Fencing." She landed a light blow and brought her glove right back to her face. "I took a class in fencing one semester."

"Didn't know that." He tucked his hand wraps on the shelf beside his gloves.

"The advice could also apply to sex." Jab, cross, round kick. She was a quick study. And a flirt.

He hadn't known that, either, since she'd never flirted with him before. "I suppose it does apply. In some cases anyway."

"Nearly all cases." Jab, cross, jab, push kick.

She had it down, the benefit of years of athletic training. He'd only had to show her once. "I can think of one time it doesn't apply."

"Yeah?"

"When two people have known each other practically their entire lives."

"I disagree." Repeating the push kick combo, she hit harder the second time. "Maybe they've known each other, but they haven't *known* each other." She went back to the first routine. "They have years of conditioning to unlearn." She sucked in a breath and did it again, only faster. "They might need to take it slower than anyone else."

"They might *need* to, but what are the chances they would?"

"Small." She sailed through the push kick combination twice, although her breathing roughened and sweat dampened her T-shirt and her hairline. "Judging from personal experience, they jump into bed and go for it, no holds barred."

"So now what? It's not like they can wave a magic wand and reverse that."

"Obviously not." She danced around the bag as she continued to groove in those two combos.

"Then what do you recommend for this imaginary couple now that they've totally loused things up?"

She paused to drag in air. "Did you bring water out here?"

"Yes." He'd automatically grabbed the filtering pitcher and two glasses and set them on the shelf. Mesmerized by Ella, he'd forgotten all about water.

"If you'd just take off my right glove, please, then I can—"

"Sure thing." He helped her with it, set it on the shelf and poured her a glass of water.

"Thanks." She closed her eyes and took several swallows.

The series of gulps sent a message straight to his groin. After last night, the simple action of Ella drinking a beverage might never be the same.

Lowering it, she gazed at him, her face pink with exertion. "I can see why you wanted this punching bag."

"It's been helpful." Gross understatement.

"I love it already and I've only worked with it for a little while."

"Longer than you think. You packed a lot into this session." Including a commentary on their relationship. "Might be time to take a break."

She nodded, polished off her water and set the glass next to the pitcher. "It would be easy to overdo this." Unlacing the other glove, she pulled it off. "It's immensely satisfying." She tucked the glove beside its mate and began unwinding the wraps.

"Yes, ma'am." He hesitated. "Listen, clearly I rushed the gate last night. No wonder you woke up disoriented."

"But you weren't disoriented." She finished one wrap and started in on the other. "How come?"

Well, now. Way to cut to the chase, Ella.

She looked up as she wound the second wrap into a neat cylinder. "Cat got your tongue?"

"You already know the answer."

She met his gaze. "Finding yourself in bed with me in the morning wasn't a shock because you've been thinking about it for a while."

"Yes." Admitting to wanting her wasn't the same as admitting he'd been in love with her all this time. He'd like to avoid detonating that land mine.

"How long?"

"I honestly don't know. I wasn't supposed to have those thoughts, so I blocked them. Or so I believed." He took a breath. "Evidently that's not your story."

"Nope. Until Saturday, you were my best friend, the brother I never had. I don't know what made me kiss you."

"Stress."

"I've been stressed when you were around and I never had that urge. I could have given you a hug, instead."

"Maybe... maybe you finally got curious."

"Maybe I did."

"Have you satisfied your curiosity?"

A slow, sensual smile touched her full lips. "Not completely."

"What's left?"

"Daytime sex."

He forgot to breathe. "But your sister—"

"We have time if we skip breakfast."

"Done."

24

Ella gave a whoop of laughter as Marsh tossed her over his shoulder for the second time. "I would have gone willingly, you know."

"Yeah, but this is more fun." He maneuvered through the back door and lengthened his stride as he headed down the hall.

"For you or me?"

"I can't speak for you, but I love it. Brings out my inner caveman."

"I kinda love it, too. Brings out my inner pinch bug." She reached down, ready to land a couple of good ones. "Except I can't get a decent grip on your booty when you're wearing these loose sweats."

"You'll get your shot when I take them off and we get busy."

"No, I won't, because I'll be on top this time."

"Looks like somebody picked up some moxie punching that bag."

"Better believe it. But first I need a shower."

"Sex first, shower after."

"But—"

"Seeing you hot and sweaty turns me on."

The pieces clicked into place. "Like after a game?"

"Except I told myself it was the cheerleaders getting me worked up. Couldn't be you. Never you."

"I was gross after a game. How could you possibly—"

"Pheromones. They're working on me right now." He edged through the bedroom door and toppled her to the unmade bed. "I want you bad, lady."

"Backatcha, cowboy." She scrambled to her knees, pulled her T-shirt over her head and tossed it... somewhere. "Take off those clothes, buster."

"Giving orders, are you?"

"Please."

"Yes, ma'am." Reaching behind him, he grabbed the back of the shirt and dragged it forward over his head and down his arms, flexing his pecs, abs and biceps in the process.

"Mmm." Distracted by his striptease, she fumbled trying to unhook her bra.

"There's a sound guaranteed to get a rise out of me." He shoved sweats and briefs down, proving his point. "Want some help with that bra?"

"Got it."

He gulped as she tossed it aside. His hungry gaze zeroed in on her breasts. "Better hurry. You're falling behind."

Her taut nipples relayed an urgent message to her womb. "I'll catch up." Leaning back on her elbows, she hooked her thumbs in the waistband of her panties and sweats, lifted her hips and pushed both as far as her knees.

He crossed to the bed. "I'll do the rest." He pulled everything off with brisk efficiency. "Damn, you smell good." His attention came to rest on her open thighs and his breath caught. "So pretty, Ellabella."

She flushed. The sunlit room hid nothing, but if she found pleasure in looking at him, he deserved to enjoy the same erotic view.

He raised his head and looked into her eyes. "Thank you."

She swallowed. "Not much mystery left."

"That's what you think." Moving to the nightstand, he opened the drawer and took out a condom. "Every time will be different." He tore the wrapper. "Every time we'll learn—"

"Don't put that on."

His eyes widened. "*What?*"

"I'll do it."

"Oh."

"Unless you don't want me to."

"Um, sure… why not?"

"Didn't mean to throw you a curve. I just thought if I'm going to be in charge…." She scooted over to make room.

"By all means." He handed her the condom and stretched out, his magnificent equipment ready and eager. But there was something going on with him.

A slight groove between his eyebrows told her was thinking again. "Hey, I don't have to—

"Are you kidding?" His frown disappeared. "I'm looking forward to it. Don't go getting cold feet on me."

"Me? Cold feet! Never."

"That's what I like to hear. You—" His breath caught as she rolled on the condom.

"You were saying?" She snapped it in place and straddled his thighs.

He grabbed a couple of pillows and stuffed them behind his head. "I was saying bring it on." His voice was a little tight, as if he might not be getting enough air. "Show me what you can do."

"I've got moves, cowboy." Bracing her palms on his chest, she splayed her fingers and pressed the tips into his warm skin. Hips hovering above her target, she leaned down and kissed him lightly with just enough tongue action to change the tempo of his breathing.

Although she might have been able to make the connection without guiding him in, she chose to reach back and make sure the moment was smooth and stress-free. For her, anyway. Marsh groaned and squeezed his eyes shut when she lowered her hips and took him up to the hilt.

She kissed her way along his stubbled jawline to the curve of his ear. "How're you doing?"

"Great."

"Assuming you don't create a problem by clenching your jaw so tight."

"I won't. Just stay still for a few seconds, okay?"

"I can do that." The occasional twitch of his cock buried deep told her he was struggling, making sure he didn't lose it so soon into the action.

She didn't want him to, either. Now that she'd womaned up and accepted the challenge of daylight sex with him, she wanted this episode to last more than five seconds.

He sighed and opened his eyes. "That's better."

"What's your special trick?"

"Special trick?"

"I figure guys must have one to keep from coming, but I've never felt comfortable enough to ask."

"They'd likely all be different."

"What's yours?" She braced herself on the mattress instead of his chest so she could lean down and make contact. Then she brushed lazily back and forth.

His breathing roughened. "I go through the skeletal structure of a horse, naming all the bones. And if you keep that up, I'll have to do it again."

She paused. "Hearing you recite that list would be amazing."

"I'm not doing it out loud."

"It would be highly entertaining."

"And exceedingly weird." He reached for another pillow and crammed it behind his head. "I realize you're the boss of this operation, but I have a hankering that requires you to change your position a little."

"Name it."

"Push up a bit and lean toward me."

"Like this?"

"Exactly like that." He cradled a breast in each palm and the conversation ended. He'd found other things to do with his mouth.

Highly effective things, too. With his thick cock buried deep and the rhythmic suction provided by his lips and tongue…. "You're gonna make me come."

His soft chuckle sent warm air over her damp skin. "So?"

"I haven't moved a muscle and yet I'm ready to—"

He brushed his thumbs lazily over her taut nipples. "When you come, and you will, you'll be moving a muscle."

"I'm supposed to be driving *you* crazy."

"Don't think you're not." His cheeks hollowed as he pulled her breast deeper into his hot mouth and began to suck.

She moaned as he created a rhythm, plucking an invisible string connecting her breast to her womb. Closer, closer… her climax arrived, a fist clenching and unclenching in time with the skillful movement of his mouth.

Her gasps became cries, nearly blotting out his deep groan. Releasing her breast, he gulped for air and muttered a string of words. Could've been salty language or a list of bones. In her current state she couldn't tell the difference.

But he hadn't come. The glorious pulsing was all hers. Breathing hard, she stared down at him. "That was new."

"Like it?"

"What do you think?"

"You made a lot of noise."

"Happy noise."

He smiled. "Thought so."

"And it's payback time."

"You don't need to take a moment to recover?"

"Not this girl." Bracing her hands on his sweaty chest, she started slow, warming up the muscles she'd use to drive him out of his ever-loving mind.

"You have that gleam in your eye."

"'Cause I'm comin' to getcha, Marsh McLintock." She increased the pace. "I'm gonna make you yell like you've never yelled before."

"Bold statement." His dark eyes glittered. "Think you can back it up?"

"I know I can. Better hang on to something. It'll be a wild ride."

"Believe I'll hang onto you." Between an upstroke and a downstroke, he slid his hands under her ass, his grip firm. "Gotcha."

"Then here we go." She pumped faster, and then faster yet. Showing off. Watching the heat in his eyes. Listening to the bed creak. He was panting, now, but so was she. And ready to come again.

His fingers tightened as he sucked in a breath and pushed upward with a bellow that made her ears ring. She followed right after, jumping on that sensual rollercoaster and yelling almost as loud as he had.

As he slowly sank back to the mattress, he maintained his hold on her backside. "Wow."

"Wow, yourself." She flashed him a grin.

He returned it. "Was that loud enough for you?"

"It'll do." She glanced at the window. "Good thing you don't have close neighbors. Your window's open."

"That's why it's open. Nobody around to hear me. Or in this case, us."

"Speaking of that, you can probably let go, now."

"I don't think so. My fingers are permanently welded to your ass."

"That could make for some socially awkward situations."

"You think?"

"I guess you could carry me into the shower and see if hot water loosens the connection. That works for jar lids."

His grin widened. "Or we could get some axle grease. That could be—" He paused. "I think I just heard the—" The chime sounded again. "Doorbell."

"Faye."

"We're screwed."

"Well, good thing your window's open." She raised her voice. "Hey, Faye! We're slightly indisposed. But come on in! We'll be out in a sec."

Faye's laughter drifted through the window. "Better take more than a sec. Judging from the yelling I heard when I climbed out of my truck, and the fascinating conversation that followed, you could both use a shower."

Ella glanced at Marsh. He shrugged. "Then we'll do that. Thanks."

"Take your time. I'll fix us some lunch."

_**25**_

Marsh gave Ella the master bath. Snatching his boots and clean clothes from the dresser and the closet, he wrapped a towel around his hips and hot-footed it down to the guest bathroom. Was he embarrassed that Faye had heard all that? Not particularly.

He'd known her as many years as he'd known Ella. She was smart, both book smart and people smart. She wasn't easily shocked.

She'd likely figured out his feelings for Ella a long time ago. His family had, so why not Ella's family? Ella was the one wearing blinders with cotton stuffed in her ears.

And he wanted to keep it that way. Didn't he? Except... when she'd told him to skip the condom, he'd immediately dived into the fantasy that she wanted a baby. With him.

Enthralled by the beauty of that fantasy, he'd lost his place in the conversation. Almost blurted out his feelings on the matter. But caution had prevailed. He'd shoved the concept aside long enough to be the playful partner she'd signed up for.

Could he keep his emotions locked down for the next few days? No telling. He'd give it a shot. Especially now that Faye was aware of the situation.

He took his time with his shave and shower. If Ella was the first one out, she could frame this any way she chose to. He'd go along with whatever she said.

By the time he left the bathroom and walked down the hall, belly laughs and giggles spilled out of the kitchen. Good sign.

The two sisters sat on either end of the table, evidently waiting for him to arrive and sit between them before they started eating. Faye had come dressed to ride, wearing jeans, a T-shirt and boots. She'd pulled her brown hair into a ponytail and her Wagon Train Cougars cap hung on the back of her chair.

She glanced at him, her green gaze amused. "Hey, Marsh."

"Hey, Faye. Have you finished talking about me? I can take my plate out to the porch if you guys need more time."

She smirked. "What makes you think we were talking about you?"

"You were both laughing your heads off."

"Because this is hysterical. I come out to entertain my sister who's all alone because you're at work, except your truck's sitting there, and—"

"I took the day off."

"So I see." She grinned. "So I heard." She gestured toward the empty chair. "Have a seat. Have some lunch."

"Thanks." He sat down and eyed a plump chicken salad sandwich and a generous serving of potato salad that was likely homemade. "Looks delicious. I'm starving."

"I can imagine. But before you dive in, I'd love to know your intentions regarding my sister."

"Faye!" Ella glared at her. "I told you what's going on. Why are you—"

"I want to hear it from him."

He took a breath. "Fair enough." He looked her in the eye and saw nothing but kindness. "When Ella and I decided she needed to stay with me, we had two goals, to keep her away from Stapleton and sort through the wedding gifts."

"How's that wedding gift sorting working out?" She gestured toward the living room, where the gifts were piled exactly the same as when they'd first come through the door.

Ella sighed. "I really don't look forward to doing it."

"Especially with such a delightful alternative."

"Even if we hadn't decided to have sex, I still wouldn't—"

"Then here's news you can use. You can skip that chore."

"Skip it?"

"Mom and Dad have been inundated with calls. Everyone wants you to keep the gifts. They bought them with you in mind, anyway. Or in some cases, handmade them."

"Like Teresa's quilt."

Faye nodded. "She was especially adamant she didn't want it back."

"That's a huge relief." Ella glanced at him. "Although now we have to take them all back to my house."

He shrugged. "No problem." Moving the presents was minor. Moving her back to her house was the part he'd rather not think about.

"So you're saying this gig started out as a rescue mission." Evidently Faye wasn't going to be distracted.

"That's right." His conscience was fairly clear on that. "We didn't... that is, we weren't thinking about—"

"That's not exactly true," Ella said. "Things changed when I kissed you."

Faye's attention swung to her sister. "*You* kissed *him*? When? You failed to mention—"

"It wasn't much of a kiss. Marsh lifted me out of the truck before we went into the reception so I wouldn't fall trying to get down. And we stood there for a minute. He'd been so great about everything and I was feeling... grateful."

"I'm gobsmacked that you made the first move. You've always sworn you'd never consider such a thing."

"Well, I—"

"Wait." Faye's eyes narrowed. "I asked you when we went back to Tyra's office if you'd ever wanted to jump his bones. You said no. And that was *after* you kissed him."

"I didn't say *no*. I said if I ever had the urge, I'd kill it because our friendship was too precious."

"So after kissing him, you killed the urge?"

"I tried to drown it in booze." She looked at him. "Thanks for your help with that project. It didn't quite work."

Faye put her napkin in her lap. "I can see this story is more complicated than I thought. We'd better start eating before Marsh keels over or the beer gets warm, whichever comes first."

"Thank you." He grasped his chilled bottle and took a reviving swig. "For the record, I had no idea that Ella was mainlining those red, white and blues because of me. I blamed Stapleton."

"We all blamed Stapleton." Faye picked up her fork.

Marsh took that as a signal he could start on the sandwich that had been calling to him for several minutes. He took a large bite. Awesome.

"And speaking of that ugly pimple on the backside of humanity," Faye dug into her potato salad. "You'll both be glad to know he's leaving town."

Marsh gulped down his food before he choked on it. Then he looked over at Ella. If Stapleton was leaving, would she move back to her house?

She frowned and gave him a quick glance. Clearly she got the subtext, too. She turned to Faye. "How do you know he's leaving?"

"He put a sign in his office window saying he's relocating. He included a website address for his new office in Billings. Maybe he hopes to hold onto some of his clients. That won't happen."

Ella fired her next question. "Is he leaving of his own accord? Because the Wenches were cooking up a—"

"According to Mom, who heard it from Desiree, the Wenches decided against following through on their plan, but they started a rumor that it might happen. Maybe that wasn't why he decided to leave, but he's a coward, so it's possible."

"Then he's definitely leaving." Marsh wished he could be happier about it.

"Looks like it."

His appetite disappeared and he put down his sandwich. He wanted Stapleton gone. But that pleasure came with a price. "Did he give a date when the office will close?"

"It's already closed."

"That's fast."

"My guess? He was eager to signal his imminent departure. He's hoping the office window sign will hold off the Wenches."

"I'm just glad he's going." Ella bit down on her sandwich.

"He hasn't left yet, though."

Ella quickly chewed and swallowed. "How do you know?"

"Brit saw him this morning at the gas station. He tried to talk to her. She couldn't drive away because she was in the middle of pumping her gas, so she pretended like he wasn't there."

Pushing aside her plate, Ella focused on her sister. "Why would he want to talk to Brit?"

"Because he can't get through to any of us since we've all blocked him, including Mom and Dad. He saw Brit and figured he might be able to deliver his message through her."

Ella stiffened. "What message?"

"That he can't leave town until he apologizes to you. He told Brit he couldn't live with himself if he didn't get a chance to do that."

Damn him! Marsh checked on Ella. If only she'd say he could wait until hell freezes over. But he could tell from her hesitation and her troubled expression that she was considering meeting with that piece of garbage.

Faye leaned toward her sister. "You don't have to see that jerk. If his conscience is bothering him — which I doubt — that's his problem."

"I know." She pulled her plate back and moved her potato salad around with her fork without taking a bite. Then she glanced up. "But if that's the only reason he's still here, then it might be the quickest way to be rid of him."

"Again, not your job."

"I agree with Faye." Marsh chose his words carefully. "I'm suspicious about his motivation. The last time I interacted with him, he was convinced he could smooth things over and get you back."

Faye nodded. "What Marsh said. We're talking about the home invasion incident, right?"

"Right. I don't trust him as far as I can throw him."

Faye smiled. "According to Ella, you could throw him pretty far."

"But that means having contact with his sorry ass. I'd rather he just drove on out of here."

Ella took a deep breath. "I wish he was already gone."

"I wish I'd never brought it up." Faye surveyed the food on the table. "Now nobody's in the mood to eat the fabulous lunch I fixed."

"It's really good, Faye. Thanks for bringing it." Marsh picked up his sandwich again. "Here's an idea. Let's forget about Stapleton, finish this great lunch and drive over to the barn. It's a good day for a ride."

"Terrific idea. I'm in." Looking relieved, Faye started eating.

Ella sent him a quick smile. "Me, too." She took a forkful of potato salad. "I can tell you made this, Faye, because you put pickle relish in it."

"Love me some pickle relish."

"She put it on everything when she was little."

"I vaguely remember that."

"Everything. On scrambled eggs, in her tomato soup, on pizza, even on toast."

"I loved it on toast. Still do."

"Seriously, sis? You're twenty-seven, not seven."

"Exactly, which means I can eat whatever I want."

"Pickle relish on toast is gross."

"I'm glad you mentioned it. I might need to make some pickle relish toast to take on our ride."

Ella looked over at him and rolled her eyes. "It's just so wrong. You do not want to see that."

He laughed. "I've never had pickle relish toast. I might love it."

"I'm sure you would." Faye winked at him. "That settles it. I'm making some for our ride. Ella, should I make enough for you?"

Ella stuck her tongue out at her sister.

The years disappeared as the little girl she used to be, the one he'd met in kindergarten, made a brief appearance. He'd been smitten at five. He still was.

He'd have to tell her that soon. And let the chips fall.

26

A long ride with Faye and Marsh filled Ella with nostalgia. They'd reminisced, teased and laughed the way they used to before Warner had come into her life. Marsh pretended to love Faye's pickle relish toast and Ella made gagging noises while they smacked their lips and moaned as if they were enjoying a five-star meal.

The past twenty-four hours hadn't changed the threesome's dynamic. Ella had worried that it might, but she could put that fear to rest.

After Marsh drove them back to the cabin, he had to return a client call, so Ella walked Faye to her truck. Twilight approached as they meandered to her parking spot. They'd invited her to stay for dinner, but she'd declined, a twinkle in her eye.

Turning toward the mountains as the shadows moved down the ridges, she spread out her arms. "Such a great spot. I love coming out here."

"Me, too. I convinced myself that life with Warner would be so wonderful I'd be fine if I only visited occasionally. What was I thinking?"

"That you wanted to start a family." Faye paused by the driver's side of her truck. "Has that changed?"

"It's just been postponed while I kick up my heels a bit. I didn't realize how boring my sex life has been. I look forward to having a lot more fun with Marsh before I settle down to being a mommy."

"Because that's when the fun stops?"

"Maybe it doesn't come to a screeching halt, but obviously when you're into diapers and two a.m. feedings, things change."

"Might partly depend on who's your baby daddy."

"It might. I'm not going to worry about finding that person now. I've always wondered how *living in the moment* works. It works like this. I'm doing it."

Faye smiled. "That's awesome. I'm happy for you."

"Thanks for being cool with everything, sis."

"Honestly? I've been expecting you guys to get involved for… geez, years."

"Not me."

"Tell me about it. Here you were hanging out with this hot cowboy and you acted like he was gender neutral."

"Not anymore."

"Finally! But I think you're kidding yourself that it won't get sappy." She opened the driver's door but didn't get in.

"It hasn't so far."

"Would it be so terrible if it did?"

"It would be weird. It's not who we are with each other. We joke around like we did today on the ride. We don't let out heartfelt sighs and exchange misty-eyed glances. We're not into that mushy stuff."

"I get that, but—"

"Sex with us is like a friendly wrestling match. With orgasms."

Faye snorted.

"And it's great exercise."

"Only you, Ella. Well, only you and Marsh, a couple of jocks geeking out on the exercise potential of sex."

"It's true, dammit!"

"I can't argue that, but I think— oh, never mind what I think. Doesn't matter. One question, though. Do you plan to let the folks know?"

"Not on purpose. I mean, if they accidentally find out, I don't care, but if I make a point of telling them, they'll think it's a big deal."

"Probably."

"Which it's not. Once Warner leaves town, I'll go home. School will start. Marsh and I won't have convenient access to each other so the whole deal might just gradually lose steam."

That brought a hoot of laughter. "I don't think so, toots. Not after what I heard earlier today."

"I was just showing off. We wouldn't keep up that pace."

"If you say so." Faye wore her *you're delusional* expression. Giving her a hug, she climbed into the cab. "Text me. Keep me in the loop."

"I will."

"Since Marsh isn't out here, yet, I guess you'll have to tell him goodbye for me. And please thank him for the ride."

"Sure thing. We need to do it again before school starts."

"I'd love that."

When her sister closed the door, Ella backed away from the truck and waved as she drove away.

"Looks like I missed her." Marsh clattered down the steps and walked over. "The call took longer than I thought."

She turned toward him. Yum and double yum. "No worries. Gave me a chance to thank her for not freaking out about us."

"Would've surprised me if she had." He slid his arms around her waist.

"She said to tell you goodbye and thanks for the ride."

He smiled. "It was fun. Like old times."

"She also asked if I was going to tell Mom and Dad about us."

"Are you?"

"Not planning on it."

"Why not?" The faint crease between his eyebrows reappeared. "They'll probably find out, anyway."

"And that's okay. But announcing it will give it more weight. They'll leap to conclusions."

"Faye didn't."

"She found out by accident."

"No kidding."

"And because she heard us going at it, she believed me when I explained we were just in it for the fun."

"That all makes sense, but let's not put on a show for your folks, okay?"

"Yeah, let's not."

"Oh, and cool about the wedding gifts, huh?"

"Very cool." She wrapped her arms around his neck. "But what will we do with all that spare time?"

"I have some ideas."

"Want to watch old Westerns?"

"My tastes must be changing." He tightened his grip. "That doesn't sound as exciting as it used to."

"Hungry?"

"Yes, ma'am." He tucked her close enough to send a strong message. "Let's go inside and see what we can find."

"Gonna toss me over your shoulder again?"

"I think we should mix things up. You toss me over your shoulder."

"Don't I wish I could. Last spring I *might* have managed it. But I'll bet you've put on thirty pounds of muscle."

"Forty."

"So if you're heavier...." She wiggled away from him. "Maybe you're slower."

"I wouldn't say—"

"Race you to the bedroom!" She took off, counting on the element of surprise to give her a decent lead. Also, running wasn't comfortable in his current state, poor guy. She made it through the door and halfway into the living room before he caught up with her.

"Gotcha." He scooped her into his arms.

"You ran even though you were—"

"It wasn't pretty, but I was motivated." Carrying her the rest of the way, he dumped her on the bed again.

It still wasn't made and the sheets held the aroma of all their hot encounters. He was right about the scent. Arousing as hell. She tugged off her boots and wrenched off her clothes.

He did the same. Then he snatched a condom from the drawer and slid in beside her, ready for action. Rolling her to her back, he moved between her thighs.

She pulled air into her lungs. "You know… in the movies… they undress each other."

"Because it's in the script." He thrust deep, lifting her off the mattress.

She gasped as her body tightened, already on the edge of a climax. "You don't like that script?"

"I might, someday." He began to move. "But when I'm craving you like this—" He pumped faster. "Undressing each other wastes time."

Wrapping her arms around him, she hung on. "I agree."

"Good." His breathing roughened. "Besides, I'd rip something."

"Understood." Body humming, she surrendered to the wild pace, rising to meet him, hooking her heels around his calves to give herself leverage.

"I like that." His hoarse voice in her ear sent shivers up her spine as he added a swivel movement with his hips.

"I like *that.*"

"Then I'll do it some more."

She had no breath for a response. Between his hip rotations and his rapid strokes, she'd given up speaking in favor of getting enough air. The sudden onset of a climax wrenched a cry from her throat, and another as the full force of a powerful orgasm engulfed her.

He rode it out and kept going, coaxing her up again. "Together," he murmured in her ear.

And so it was, their moments of release blending and spiraling in a sensual dance that made her dizzy with pleasure.

At the peak of her climax, when the air shimmered and the blood pounded hot and fierce through her veins, she called out his name.

He answered, saying hers with a rich undercurrent of emotion that burrowed deep. No one had ever said her name quite like that. Then again, no one had ever given her a moment filled with such indescribable bliss.

She'd leaped into this adventure for the fun of it. Somewhere along the way, fun had become something far more potent. She hadn't planned on that. But whatever this was, she could say one thing for sure. It wasn't sappy.

27

As Marsh's breathing slowed and his heart stopped pounding like a runaway horse, he gazed at Ella lying beneath him. She looked right back at him, her eyes heavy-lidded with satisfaction, her rosy lips parted, her cheeks flushed, her golden hair spread across the pillow.

"You're beautiful."

Her breath caught and her eyes widened. "What?"

Clearly he'd surprised her with that comment. Couldn't very well take it back. Couldn't think of a joke. Gradually her startled expression shifted to wariness.

He'd screwed up. Better exit the scene and figure out what to do next. "I'll go take care of the condom."

"Okay."

Turning on a light, he disposed of the condom and washed up, which included meeting his sorry self in the mirror. "Nice going, genius."

"Are you talking to yourself in there?"

"Yes, ma'am." Grabbing a towel, he dried off.

She appeared in the doorway. "What about?"

"I think you know."

"Faye warned me it could get sappy."

His chest tightened. "What did you say to that?"

"That it would feel weird."

"Does it?"

She nodded.

He gulped. Made himself ask the question. "Why?"

"Because that's not who we are. That's not how we relate to each other. We're best friends. We're not...."

"Lovers?" His chest ached so bad. Probably his heart cracking.

Her answer was a whisper, but clear despite that. "Right."

He covered a gasp of pain with a cough. "Tell you what. We need to talk this out. And not in here."

"Yeah, the bathroom isn't—"

"Neither is the bedroom. Let's put on some clothes and sit on the porch, get some fresh air."

"Sounds good."

Nothing sounded good, but the porch meant they'd sit side-by-side in the rockers. Might be better if he didn't look at her while he made his confession. Judging from her reaction so far, she wouldn't like hearing it.

Fabric rustled in the silence as they put on the clothes they'd recently thrown off. And the boots. He swept a hand toward the door.

On the way down the hall, he asked if she wanted something to drink. He had to clear his throat twice to make the offer.

"No, thanks." She marched through the house and out the front door as if she might keep on going and walk all the way back to town.

She left the chair closest to the door for him and took the one next to it.

He'd managed to hold it together a mere twenty-four hours. Less than that, really. What a dreamer he'd been. He'd figured on days, maybe even weeks of enthusiastic sex with Ella.

He would have settled for that. Then again, if he'd been given weeks, he might have made some inroads. Instead he'd careened into a ditch in less than twenty-four hours.

"You're thinking, again." She said it gently, almost tenderly.

"Just wondering if there's any way out of the ditch I've landed in."

"We've landed in. I should have seen this coming."

"It didn't have to. I meant exactly what I said when I suggested this yesterday afternoon. I swear that was my intention, for us to enjoy great sex with no romantic BS. I know you're not in love with me, so—"

"Are you in love with me?"

"Yes, God help me, I am. Have been for years. I've never admitted it, not to anyone and least of all to myself."

"Did you know you were in love with me when you made this suggestion?"

"Yes, but I—"

"Marsh!" Her voice was drenched in misery. "You set yourself up for a fall!"

"That's not how I saw it. I knew we'd be good in bed. Even if you weren't in love with me, we could still share some extraordinary sex. I didn't want to go to my grave never having that experience with you. Maybe that was selfish, but that was my motivation."

She took a deep breath and blew it out. "I'll bet I know when your plan started falling apart."

"When you told me not to put on the condom."

"You thought I meant not to use it at all, didn't you?"

"What can I say? You'd admitted you chose to marry Warner so you could start having babies. Then I delivered Beau and Jess's little girl. I had babies on the brain."

"What a mess. And it's my fault."

"No way."

"Oh, yeah, it is. Why couldn't I have continued to think of you as a Ken doll with no genitals?"

"*That's* the image you've—"

"Yes! And it's worked great for years. But when my wedding went up in smoke, so did that image. I fought it. Boy, did I fight it. I didn't want to want you. But I did and here we were living together, and you came up with what I thought was a great workaround."

"It was. It could've been."

"No! It was wrong from the get-go!" She pushed out of her chair and began to pace and wave her arms in the air. "You know you can't keep things from me. You've never been able to. What made you think you could keep me from finding out you're in love with me?"

"Stupidity?"

"Yessir."

"Okay." He pushed out of his chair. "My ass is cooked, so I'm going for broke. You used to think of me as a dickless wonder, correct?"

"No, that's too harsh. I just smudged out that part of—"

"Details." He paced to the opposite end of the porch and turned. "Then, you go through an emotional experience, and suddenly I'm man candy."

"Something like that."

"You like having sex with me, but you're not in love with me. You love me as a friend, a pal you hang out with and recently had some great sex with. Am I nailing it so far?"

"Look, I know where you're going with this, and I'm telling you right now, I can't imagine you and me married with kids."

"So what? A couple of weeks ago you couldn't imagine me with a penis. Why couldn't you someday switch me into the lover, husband, baby-daddy category? Why is that impossible?"

She stared at him, her body quivering with tension. "I suppose it isn't, but—"

"Aha! What if it happened tomorrow?"

"It won't."

"Or next week?"

"What if it never happened at all?"

"What if you married me because I'm a great catch and I'd be happy to give you babies?

Because if that switch is possible, you sure don't want it happening when you're married to some loser who probably wouldn't have the excellent gene pool I can offer you."

"You're crazy."

"Think about it, Ellabella. You could do a lot worse. In fact, you almost did." He headed for the door. "I'll take the guest room tonight."

28

Ella stayed out on the porch, walking back and forth as darkness fell and the crickets tuned up. Marsh had never yelled at her like that. Was he on the back porch pounding on his punching bag? Quite likely.

He'd been angry with her before, just like she'd been angry with him many times over the years. But just now he'd gone past angry. He was furious.

With good reason. Her stubborn mindset made no logical sense. If she could make the switch from sexless buddy to hot sex partner, what was stopping her from making the next transition?

She should accept his proposal, even though he'd tossed it out in the middle of his rant. Why couldn't she just agree to marry him? Because... she'd lose her best friend.

That argument made no sense, either. He'd said their friendship was bulletproof. But was it? Had she already lost her best friend and wasn't willing to face it?

And what was that delicious aroma coming from inside the house? Was he *cooking*? Her stomach rumbled. How inconvenient. People in crisis weren't supposed to be hungry.

When he'd said he'd spend the night in the guest room, he should have gone straight there — well, after smacking his punching bag around — and not come out until morning. Her mom and her girlfriends had claimed it was true. After an argument, most men retreated like a bear going into his cave to nurse his wounds.

Well, this bear was whipping up something in the kitchen that made her mouth water. When her stomach cramped with hunger, she gave up, went inside and braved the kitchen.

Temptation stood by the stove, shirt hanging open, butt looking amazing in those snug jeans while he tended to something in the frying pan. He glanced over his shoulder. "Want some?"

Oh, Marsh. He'd never looked sexier. "What is it?"

"Sloppy Joes. I made enough to share, just in case."

"I'd love some. Thanks."

"How about getting us some chips? They're in the—"

"I know where they are." She walked into the kitchen and opened a cupboard that was a safe distance from the hot cowboy currently making Sloppy Joes. She opened the bag and set it on the table. "Do you have plates?"

"Got two here by the stove."

"Two? How'd you know I'd be in?"

"Seriously, Ella? Why do you think I made this? It's a peace offering. I yelled at you a while ago and I didn't want to leave things like that between us. I don't yell at you. It's not cool."

"Why not? You made a valid point and my position isn't at all logical."

"Doesn't matter. I value our friendship. Like I've told you about a million times, it's bulletproof."

"Still? After all this?"

He set buns on the plates and began dishing the Sloppy Joes. "Marry me or not. That's up to you, although I strongly suggest you do. In any case, I'll be in your life until one of us croaks. That's the way of it." He turned around, a plate in each hand. "Want a beer?"

She was scared to death she was about to cry. She swallowed. "I won't marry you, but I would love a beer."

"Great." He set the plates on the table. "We need to strategize next steps."

"Next steps for what?"

He took two chilled bottles out of the fridge and nudged it closed with his knee. "For how you're going to handle Stapleton. Now that I've had some time to think about it, it's pretty clear to me he's not likely to leave town without seeing you, so—"

"You think I should meet with him?"

"I don't think you *should*, but if he's determined to make it happen, let's make it as safe as possible for you." He twisted the tops off both bottles and set one at each place. He'd put them across the table from each other.

"Why did you seat us so far apart?"

"Because I want to make peace and figure out this Stapleton plan, but I don't want to have sex with you. Well, I do, but it's not in our best interests."

"Agreed." Even though she could eat him up with a spoon. "Thank you for making dinner."

"You're welcome. I'd help you into your chair, but...."

"Don't trouble yourself. I understand. I feel the same way."

"Just to be clear, what way is that?"

"I want to have sex with you, but I realize it's not in our best interests."

"Then I didn't kill your fascination with my body with that diatribe on the porch?"

"If only." She heaped chips on her plate.

"Then you're back in the not-wanting-to-want-me mode?"

"That about describes it."

He smiled. "Good to know."

"Don't you dare look smug about that!"

"I'll look smug if I want to." He gestured toward the food. "I can cook and I'm good in the sack. I would mention that I can clean toilets, but I don't want to oversell myself."

She laughed. Couldn't help it. "What am I going to do with you?"

"You could—"

"Never mind. Rhetorical question." She picked up her very messy Sloppy Joe and took a big bite. Juice ran over her fingers. Once she'd chewed and swallowed, she licked them clean. "Delicious."

"You test my resolve, Ella Bradley."

She glanced up. Heat flared in his dark eyes. "Don't blame me. You're the one who fixed these."

"It wasn't a bad choice. Just a helluva tempting one." He took a long swallow of his beer and set it back on the table. "What's the best plan for meeting Stapleton?"

"A public place."

"Good."

"Let people know what I'm doing."

"Also good. Can you make it in the evening? I'd like to be there, if you're okay with that. I'll cancel appointments if I have to, but—"

"I'll make it in the evening. But I wouldn't want him to see you."

"I'll stay out of sight. Any thoughts on where?"

"Probably the Buffalo."

"Good choice. We can have Clint and Rance there that night. Inside is no problem, but my guess is he'll try to lure you into his SUV."

"Why?"

"You bruised his ego. He may say he needs to apologize, but I don't buy it."

"I don't really believe he wants to clear his conscience before he leaves town, either."

"The man I rousted from your living room isn't the apologizing type. Clint and Rance can cover the interior, but I'll station myself in sight of his vehicle. Then you'll have backup."

"Thank you."

"Now eat your Sloppy Joe before it gets cold. Or I get ideas. More ideas."

"All right." She tucked into the meal, her senses tuned to the man at the other side of the table who was busy eating his meal, too. Sex could make a person hungry for food. Food could make a person hungry for sex.

When she'd finished her Sloppy Joe and was down to a few chips and the rest of her beer, she glanced across the table. "I need to go home tomorrow."

"I know."

"You have clients."

"I can take you early. The first one's not until ten."

"I have a million wedding presents stacked in your living room."

"Is it important to you to get them back under your roof?"

"No."

"Then we can leave them for now." He gazed at her across the table. "I don't like the idea of you going back to your house while Stapleton's still in town."

"I'm not easy about it, either. That's why I want to set the meeting for tomorrow night. He should agree, given what he told Brit. Then he'll have no excuse not to leave town the next day."

"Uh-huh." Marsh took a swig of his beer.

"You don't think he will?"

"I hope for everyone's sake he does. I'm not counting on it."

And on that cheery thought... She polished off her beer and pushed back her chair. "Dinner was wonderful. I'll help you clean up."

"That won't work for me." He stood. "Not to be pushy, but I need you to skedaddle."

"I could just—"

"Go to your room, please. And stay there."

"But—"

"I've made it through the peace-keeping meal and the discussion about Stapleton, but the longer I look at you, the more I want to join you in that big bed tonight."

She was tempted to invite him in. But he was in love with her. It wasn't just fun and games with them anymore. If she had no intention of giving him what he really wanted, then leading him on would be cruel.

Leaving her plate and empty bottle on the table, she stood. "Then goodnight. Sleep well."

His voice was husky. "You, too."

Walking out of that kitchen was tough. All her instincts urged her to throw herself into his arms. He'd cave, no question. And she'd hate herself in the morning.

29

Marsh's night was hell and the next day wasn't an improvement. Taking Ella home made his stomach churn. He did a security walk-through to convince himself the place hadn't been breached in her absence. She promised to lock up after him and stay put until she met Stapleton at the Buffalo.

He didn't kiss her goodbye. Somehow he managed to avoid touching her at all. Yep, total hell. He drove away in a rotten mood.

His day was packed with client appointments. He used the half-hour he'd allowed for lunch to sit in his truck and call his mother. He took a chance calling her on a workday, but she picked up.

"Hey, Mom. Got a minute?"

"I have about fifteen. You caught me on my lunch break. What's up?"

He quickly filled her in on the Warner plan. "I was hoping you'd help me contact folks, but it sounds like you're—"

"In the middle of a crucial chapter? I am, but I'll put it aside. Time to rally the Wenches."

"The Wenches? Please tell me you won't go through with that gonzo plan to—"

"No, son. I talked them out of that scheme, but Warner doesn't know that. He thinks we still have it ready to go and just need an excuse to pull the trigger. If the Wenches show up at the Buffalo and we're conveniently seated near his table—"

"He'll think twice about messing with Ella. Good strategy. I'm also looking for muscle, just in case he tries to get her into his SUV."

"I'll alert Sky. He'll pass the word to your brothers and Angie."

"We'd better leave Beau out of it, though."

"I wouldn't. He'll want to be there after you charged to his rescue. Jess and Mav will be okay for a couple of hours. Or Penny can run over."

He smiled. "Mav? She has a nickname already?"

"Jess says they're a one-syllable family."

"But legally she's Jessica, three syllables."

"But nobody calls her that. Until Maverick learns to talk and can take matters into her own hands, she'll be Mav."

"Alrighty, then." He couldn't wait to tell Ella. She'd laugh at that. Except they had no plans to see each other. She'd probably hear it from someone else.

"Are you going to call Ella's folks?"

"She's making that call, and contacting Faye and Brit. The Buffalo will have a crowd for dinner."

"That show of support should cool that idiot's jets while he's in the restaurant, but you're smart to have plenty of backup outside. I write scenes like this all the time with unpredictable characters. Anyone who doesn't take precautions with this type ends up in big trouble."

"Which we all learned from your books."

"I just hope tonight marks the final chapter of this miserable story."

"I hope so, too. Thanks for the help."

"Of course. Just one question, if I may."

"Sure."

"Does Ella know you're in love with her?"

He hesitated. "She does, now."

"Oh, dear. You didn't say that with your happy voice."

"Mom."

"Well, you didn't. It was a disaster, wasn't it?"

"Yes, ma'am."

"I'm sorry."

"Me, too. I'll... we'll talk soon. 'Bye, Mom."

"'Bye, son."

He disconnected and stared out the window at the Sapphires, cool and green. Yesterday at this time he'd been mounted on Diablo, soaking up the fun of a trail ride with Ella and Faye while anticipating another magical night with Ella.

Some of it had been magical. Most of it had been crap. But the mountains hadn't changed. They would soon, though.

Another month and the yellows and reds would appear. Ella would be teaching her PE classes at WHS and coaching basketball. He'd go to the games and take her out for pizza afterward, like he'd been doing ever since she'd accepted the job when Coach Blake retired.

Could they go back to the easy friendship they'd had before? Not at first. They'd have to work through some awkward moments. But he'd make sure they did, because life without Ella in it was unthinkable.

* * *

Ella took deep breaths, working hard to control her jitters. Her online exchange with Dinah hadn't helped. But she was glad she'd taken time to make that connection and thank the woman who'd kept her from marrying a cheater.

Dinah's comments weren't surprising, but disturbing, nevertheless. She'd called Warner a snake and had advised Ella not to meet with him under any circumstances. She didn't believe for a minute that he was filled with guilt and remorse.

Neither did she. But she wanted him out of town, so she'd push her way through this evening.

Most of the parking spaces in front of the Buffalo were taken. Then she lucked out. The backup lights flashed on a silver truck parked near the entrance. Wait, wasn't that Sky's truck?

The driver stuck his hand out the window and gave her a wave. Definitely Sky. Marsh had planned to rally the troops. Evidently Sky had nabbed the parking spot and held it for her. He drove down the street and she pulled right in.

His kind gesture warmed her as if he'd personally given her a hug. She'd be the one facing Warner, but she wouldn't be alone. Marsh was stationed somewhere in the shadows, keeping watch. Rance would be behind the bar and Clint would be playing the genial host, making his presence known. Her parents were probably already seated at a table with Faye and Brit.

Grabbing her purse from the seat next to her, she climbed down, took another deep breath and walked toward the entrance. She could do this.

Welcooome toooo the Buffaloooo. The wooden mascot's recorded voice greeted her as she stepped inside. She made a quick survey. Warner was at a table for two by the dance floor. Her folks sat at a four-top toward the middle of the room.

Then she spotted the Wenches, all looking at her and giving her a subtle thumbs-up sign. Excellent. A show of force by the Wenches should make Warner sweat. This might turn into a fun evening, after all.

Cecily hurried toward her. "He's here."

"I see that."

"I so wanted to spill something on him, but Clint told me I wasn't allowed."

"If all goes according to plan, you won't ever have to serve him again."

"That would be lovely. He makes my skin crawl. Ready to go?"

"Yes." She followed Cecily. The closer they came to Warner, the uglier he became. The bruise on his cheek had faded a bit but the makeup he'd used still didn't completely disguise it. The blond hair and blue eyes she'd once called handsome made her sick to her stomach. He smiled and waved. She didn't respond.

As Cecily led her over to him, he left his chair and rounded the table.

Ella shook her head and made a shooing motion. "Sit down."

He shrugged and resumed his seat. "Suit yourself."

Cecily touched her shoulder. "Can I bring you anything from the bar?"

"No, thank you. I'll just have water. And I'm ready to order." She eyed Warner's fancy-dancy cocktail in a stemmed glass. Half of it was already gone. "I'll just have a bowl of chili, please, Cecily."

Warner rolled his eyes. "Aw, c'mon, Ella. I'm trying to apologize, here. Let me buy you a decent meal before I ride off into the sunset."

"I'm not really hungry." So true.

"Cecily, bring us two steaks with all the fixings. Mine's medium, hers is medium rare. And two more of these things." He gestured toward the stemmed glass. "If she doesn't drink hers, I will."

Eyebrows raised, Cecily glanced at her.

"He can have both drinks. And I'll have the chili." No way was she letting him take control of this situation, but if he got drunk, so much the better. Easier to get his *ride off into the sunset* comment to stick.

Cecily left, and Warner looked across the table, his gaze assessing. "I'm glad I ordered you a drink. You look uptight."

So did he. The Dutch courage must not be working. He leaned against the chair in a careless pose, but his rigid jaw and the slight tremble of his hand as he picked up the drink gave him away.

"The place is busy tonight."

"Don't think I can't see what you've done, bringing your parents and sister in. You probably have something to do with Desiree McLintock's posse showing up, too."

"I did let my folks know we were meeting here tonight. For some mysterious reason, they don't trust you and wanted to be on hand, just in case."

"Ridiculous."

"As for the Wenches, I have nothing to do with that."

"They're trying to intimidate me. Pathetic."

"Word has it they succeeded, and that's why you closed your office."

"That's bull. The company wants me in Billings to prop up a failing agency."

"Then you're definitely going?"

"Sure am. You're the last loose end I need to tie up. I was—"

The band launched into a two-step.

He switched gears. "Want to dance?"

"No. I want to hear what you were about to say."

"I was a bastard, Ella. To be fair, Dinah threw herself at me, but—"

"That's not how she tells it."

His eye began to twitch. "You talked to her?"

"We connected online. She's not a fan. And she says you came after her, not the other way around."

"Well, she would say that, wouldn't she? She doesn't want to admit that her little scheme to coax me into breaking my engagement didn't work." He gave her a soulful look. "In the end, I came back to you, Ella."

"Lucky me."

"You're not ready to forgive my little lapse, are you?"

"Oh, I am, because you did me the favor of cheating *before* we got married. And you picked a woman who felt some compassion for the woman who was about to marry your philandering self. I come out the winner in this story."

"You are a winner, Ella, and I messed up, big time. Did you just say you forgive me?"

"Yes, with a whole bunch of qualifiers attached."

"I don't care about the qualifiers. I'm latching onto the forgiveness part." He leaned toward her. "That makes me so happy. I—"

"Ah, Warner Stapleton. I thought I saw you over here." Clad in her signature orange, Teresa approached the table. "I thought you'd be gone by now."

Warner's eye twitched again. "Tomorrow. I'm leaving tomorrow."

"See that you do." Teresa gave Ella's arm a squeeze and left.

Warner took a hefty swallow of his drink. "They're harmless."

"Sure they are." Ella glanced over at the Wenches' table where Teresa was exchanging high-fives with her buddies. Chances were good each of them would drop by eventually.

Turned out she was right. As Warner tried to eat his steak dinner and convince her he was worth keeping, the Wenches took turns dropping by the table and inquiring about his plans.

Eventually, he snapped. Tossing his napkin on the table, he drained the third drink, fished in his wallet and threw a wad of bills on the table. "I've had enough. Let's get out of here."

"What?" Alarm bells flashed.

"I have something I need to give you. It's in my car."

More alarm bells. "I'll wait here while you go get it."

"I'd rather not come back in here. Those Wenches creep me out."

"What could you possibly have to give me?"

"I found a matching cup for your toddler Winnie-the-Pooh dish set to replace the one that lost a handle."

"I forgot all about that."

"I didn't. It was important to me. I pictured using it for our kids, but..." He sighed. "I royally screwed up so that won't be happening."

"No, it won't." Why on Earth had he made the effort to replace that cup?

"I regret that more than I can say. In any case, you gave me the whole set — cup with the missing handle, bowl and plate. I found the match in Florida and bought a special box where it all fits. I was planning to give it to you on our wedding night."

"Oh."

"Just come outside with me. I'll go get the box and bring it back to you. Then we'll be done."

She hesitated. The guy wanted to return her Winnie-the-Pooh dishes. They weren't expensive, but they had lots of sentimental value.

Yes, he was still trying to manipulate her, but Marsh was out there, probably with a couple of his brothers.

If she said no, Warner might use it as an excuse to hang around. Or worse, he might try to drop the box off at her house. That would be bad for many reasons. If she agreed to go outside, she'd have Marsh to watch her back and could have the added satisfaction of watching Warner drive away. She wanted that. "I'll walk out with you."

30

Marsh's phone pinged with a text from Clint. *She just left with him.*

He checked the sidewalk. *I see them.* He sent a group text alerting his siblings hidden in the shadows between Stapleton's SUV and the Buffalo. They'd all wanted in, each of them eager for an excuse to pop Stapleton in the chops. Or in the gut, in the knees, whatever was handy.

Ella walked beside Stapleton but maintained at least a foot between them. Her purposeful stride was achingly familiar. Among a million other things, he loved the way she walked — shoulders back, chin up, eyes forward.

He'd stationed himself right across the sidewalk from Stapleton's SUV. Sky and Beau weren't far. Bret and Gil had fanned out, ready to leap on the SUV's running board if Stapleton managed to get Ella inside and start driving.

Angie and Lucky stayed on the move, ready to dash to the rescue wherever they were needed.

When Ella and Stapleton reached the SUV, Marsh froze. Ella glanced toward his hiding place. Did she see him? Sense him? She gave no sign.

Stapleton opened the SUV, took out a box and laid it on the hood. Ella reached for it. And Stapleton grabbed her.

Marsh surged forward.

"Oh, hell no!" Ella's battle cry stopped him.

Her next moves didn't happen in slow motion, but later he'd swear they did. She spun away from Stapleton and brought her hands up. As he lunged toward her, she punched him in the face. She followed with a round kick, landed another punch that snapped his head back, and ended her routine with a push kick to the balls that brought him to his knees.

The McLintock siblings watched in wide-eyed fascination.

"Get out of town, loser!" Panting, Ella snatched the box from the hood of the car and backed away. "Apology, my ass! Dinah was right. Marsh was right! If you ever come back, expect more of the same! Get the hell out of here."

"Ella," Lucky said gently, "he can't walk right now, let alone drive."

Her attention swung to him. Then she turned in a circle, taking in the McLintocks gathered to offer protection she clearly hadn't required. "Thanks. Thanks to all of you for being here. Maybe you could help him into the driver's seat. He'll recover eventually."

Bret and Gil nodded and transferred a moaning Stapleton from the pavement to his vehicle.

Ella turned again. "Marsh? Where are you?"

"Here." He stepped forward.

"Thank you for organizing the backup."

"Doesn't seem like you needed it."

"Only because of what you taught me." She took short, quick breaths. "Thank you for that, too."

"You're welcome."

Glancing down, she straightened the knit top she'd worn, lifted her chin and managed a wobbly smile. "Didn't get my shirt dirty."

"Well done."

She took a longer, deeper breath. "Okay, everybody, back to the Buffalo!" She held the box against her side and thrust her free hand in the air. "Drinks are on me!"

* * *

That kind of emotional upheaval could have created a transformation in Ella. Marsh liked his odds for that happening after she'd beaten the crap out of the man who'd wronged her, the man who'd tried to dupe her a second time.

Unfortunately, no switch had been thrown in Ellabella, judging from her radio silence after that dramatic night. He discussed it with his mom and she counseled patience. He debated it with Clint, who advised him to storm the barricades, maybe even stand outside her window with a boombox.

He wasn't a storm-the-barricades kind of guy, so he went with his mom's advice. Patience was his superpower.

Or maybe not. Waiting for a signal from the woman he loved became the kind of slow torture that could lead to madness. On top of it, the damn wedding presents remained stacked in his living room. His reading corner was destroyed. Not that he was reading, but still.

The night he decided to make Sloppy Joes was a new low. They reminded him of her, and he was so pathetic that it was enough to justify creating the meal. He even made too much, as if the aroma of Sloppy Joes simmering in the frying pan would travel all the way into town.

Then she drove up. Was he hallucinating? But when he walked out on the porch, there was her truck. She climbed out of it and came toward him with a box in her hand. It looked familiar.

"What is that?" Brilliant. How about hello, glad to see you, how've you been?

"It's a Winnie-the-Pooh toddler dish set. There's a cup, a bowl and a plate."

"It looks like the same box Warner gave you the night you kicked him in the balls." Talk about a romantic conversation. He was a real Romeo.

"It's the same box." She climbed the steps. "I smell Sloppy Joes."

"I was making some in case you came over."

She stared at him.

"Kidding."

"Do you have enough for me?"

"Yes."

"Am I invited?"

"Yes."

"Great." She walked past him and into the house, still carrying the box. "I could use a Sloppy Joe, chips and a beer."

"I'm out of chips."

"Then a Sloppy Joe and a beer."

"That I have."

"Then let's eat. We'll talk afterward."

"About what?"

"These dishes."

"If they have anything to do with Stapleton, I'd rather not."

"Not really. Sort of, but not the important part."

"You know, I've been wishing you'd come over, but I was hoping you'd make a little more sense than this."

"I will. But after I explain everything, you'll forget about food. It's better to eat first."

Explaining sounded like a good thing. A tiny flame of hope flickered in the dreary wasteland he'd lived in for days. "I'll dish us up."

She helped him get the meal on the table and filled him in on her plans for the school year. She asked about Beau and Jess's baby and he told her Mav was clearly a genius child who would rule the family one day. Ella hadn't heard about the one-syllable concept and sure enough, she laughed when he told her.

He ate fast. Fortunately she didn't take a lot of time finishing her meal, either. "Want another beer?"

"Sure."

He tried not to attach too much importance to that, but she was careful about drinking and driving. Accepting a second beer might mean... no, he'd be wise not to make assumptions.

Testing the Cowboy's Resolve

He set two chilled bottles on the table. "Tell me about these dishes."

"They're mine from when I was a kid. I got Winnie-the-Pooh and Faye got Raggedy Ann and Andy. My folks kept my set for me to use for my kids, but the handle on my cup was broken, probably by me." She pulled the dishes out of the box, included the cup with no handle and the one with a handle.

"Why did Stapleton have them?"

"When I showed him the dishes, he offered to look for a replacement for the cup without a handle. I gave him the whole set, I guess because I wanted to keep it all together. Or a gesture of trust. I was trusting back then. Anyway, he found the replacement cup and that was his bait to get me down to his vehicle."

"Clever on his part."

"It worked to lure me outside, but when he grabbed me, and I realized he'd used my Winnie-the-Pooh dishes as bait, I… I kinda went berserk."

"You were amazing. But why bring the dishes here?"

She met his gaze. "They belong here."

"You're giving them to me?"

"Yes, because I can trust you with them." She scooted her chair closer. "I couldn't trust him but I can trust you." She choked up a little. Then she sniffed and went on. "You're the only one, Marsh. I couldn't see it before, but I can't have babies with anyone but you. Will you please marry me?"

He stopped breathing. Then he gasped for air. "But… you're not in love with me. You can't marry someone just to have babies when you're not in—"

"But I am in love with you."

Don't question it, dude. But he did, He had to. "What about keeping me as a best friend? I thought I couldn't be both."

"That's what tied me in knots. I thought if I fell in love with you, then I wouldn't have a best friend anymore, a confidant. If I married you, who would I talk to when we had issues?"

He groaned in frustration. "*Me*, Ella. You'd talk to me, like we've been doing for almost twenty-five years."

She made a face. "I finally figured that out."

He couldn't decide whether to laugh or swear. "If we'd only had this conversation—"

"But we couldn't! On top of it, I thought being in love was like coming down with something — you got all these fluttery feelings and had to be with the person twenty-four-seven and all the romantic BS I've heard all my life."

"That can happen."

"But not with us. We know each other too well and we're not sentimental types."

"You're sentimental about those dishes."

"Okay, maybe with some things I'm—"

"And your Wagon Train Cougars cap."

"Yes, but—"

"And when you get right down to it, you're sentimental as hell about our friendship."

She stared at him. "You're right." She sucked in a breath. "It's complicated."

"No, it's not. Come here." He stood and pulled her out of her chair. "I get you and you get me." He tugged her close. "Simple as that. We're made for each other."

She got choked up again. "It's true." She gazed up at him, blinking away tears. "That's why sex was so much fun."

"*Is* so much fun." He cupped her face and stroked her damp cheek gently with his thumb. "And could we please call it making love from now on? Because it's more than just—"

"I know." She sniffed again. "But will we still laugh when we're making love?"

"God, I hope so."

"That settles it. Will you marry me, please?"

"Yes, Ellabella." He held very still, memorizing the shimmer of happy tears in her eyes, the warmth of her body cradled against his, the thud of his happy heart. "A thousand times yes. I love you more than I can ever say. And if that's too sappy for you, then—"

"It's not." She hugged him tight. "Marsh McLintock, I'm in love with you. I'm so in love with you that I could gobble you up."

He smiled. "Music to my ears."

"You're more appealing than your Sloppy Joes, and that's saying a lot, because I absolutely adore your Sloppy Joes."

"Careful. Getting sappy."

"I kinda like it."

"I kinda do, too. What do you say we take the sappy up a notch and kiss to seal the deal?"

"We probably should. This has been a long time coming."

"No kidding." He captured her lips like a man dying of thirst. The wait was over.

* * * * *

Coming this holiday season!

**ROCKING THE COWBOY'S CHRISTMAS, book
four in the Rowdy Ranch series!**

* * * * *

New York Times bestselling author Vicki Lewis Thompson's love affair with cowboys started with the Lone Ranger, continued through Maverick, and took a turn south of the border with Zorro. She views cowboys as the Western version of knights in shining armor, rugged men who value honor, honesty and hard work. Fortunately for her, she lives in the Arizona desert, where broad-shouldered, lean-hipped cowboys abound. Blessed with such an abundance of inspiration, she only hopes that she can do them justice.

For more information about this prolific author, visit her website and sign up for her newsletter. She loves connecting with readers.

VickiLewisThompson.com

Lightning Source UK Ltd.
Milton Keynes UK
UKHW010648100822
407113UK00003B/1153